T.M. Cooks is the pen name of the following collaborative writing team. The contributors are:

- Abbie Tracey McInaw

- Batoul Ali

- Elaine J. McLeish

- Ellie B.

- Emily C. A. Johnson

- Esther Meldrum

- Georgia White

- Meghan Lynch

- Ruby A. Redmond

- Sanuthi De Silva

with cover design by the writers. The project was lead by:

- Ashley Waner

- Yingchen Liu

The group cheerfully acknowledges the wonderful help given by:

- Douglas Hogg

Most importantly, we'd like to thank our funders, the Scottish Government School Library Improvement Fund.

Its been a wonderful opportunity, and everyone involved has been filled with incredible knowledge and enthusiasm. Finally, we would like to thank all staff at Bellahouston Academy for their support in releasing our novelists from lessons for a full week.

The group started to plan out their novel at 9.15am on Monday 15th May 2023 and completed their last proof reading at 3.30pm on Friday 19th May 2023.

We are incredibly proud to state that every word of the story, every idea, every chapter and yes, every mistake, is entirely their own work. No teachers, parents or other students touched a single key during this process, and we would ask readers to keep this in mind. We are sure you will agree that this is an incredible achievement. It has been a true delight and privilege to see this group of young people turn into professional novelists in front of our very eyes.

Rings of Ice

T. M. Cooks

Contents

Chapter 1

For Peace

A wedding; a joyous occasion for all, usually. But not in this instance.

The marriage of Prince Louis Von Lothbrok III and Princess Aven Laila Benedict was the result of two war torn kingdoms- Anathena and Caligo- making a stab at peace and uniting the people of their lands. Arrangements had been made hastily for a winter wedding, a week after the two kingdoms declared a truce. A week after the 16 year war came to a close.

No time like the present, after all.

News of the occasion had spread like wildfire among the people- sparking a sense of hope, and a fire of excitement.

Consequently, Prince Louis now stood before a vast alter, awaiting his bride, far from thrilled. The furthest from it. He couldn't have dreaded it more. The wedding was nothing more than a nuisance, in his eyes, sparking argument upon argument with his father on the matter.

Louis' face was blank, unreadable, as he stood tall and still- looking remarkably as though he were one of the grand statues that lined the sides of the wedding hall. His dark brown hair- normally untouched- had been combed and pinned to perfection. His royal blue suite was tailored perfectly and fit him like a glove. He looked like the perfect husband. In theory.

Inside his mind, however, was far from perfect. A flurry of thoughts and worries filled his mind, many of those began with "what if?"

His eyes danced around the wedding hall. It had been decorated to match the colour of his suite. It was breathtakingly gorgeous. Objectively so, Louis paired it no notice. After all- it wasn't even a real marriage. It was more like an agreement. That was all it was.

All it would ever be.

Aven's mother, his father, the nanny that had practically raised him and thousands of others were seated before him- watching and waiting with the anticipation of a child-for the ceremony to start.

He glanced towards his best friend of twenty years or so ;Demiar.

Demiar gave him an encouraging half smile, as

though to consoling him. Louis let his gaze wander to the empty space beside his friend, where Demiar's sister, -Louis' great love- Kali should have been sitting. That was the worst part about the damned wedding: it had stripped Louis of the only girl he'd ever truly loved or even cared about. Louis took a deep breath in - stabling himself- before turning his attention to the wedding at hand. He would not allow himself to torture his mind any further over the girl he could never have.

The orchestra began to play a few soft notes, the buzz of excitement quieted and the guests stood, spinning eagerly in turn to face the grand oak doors.

As the doors opened they allowed rays of sunlight to shine through the hall. He knew that in a few moments Aven would walk down that aisle, and the two would meet for the first time in sixteen years.

The music slowed to a gentle melody, and then there she was.

Aven.

Louis simply couldn't help but gaze at her. Her dress was beautifully embroidered, the silk pooling at her feet, and the lace bodice of her gown hugging her figure. Her white hair lay in neat curls against her back and a grand tiara sat proudly atop her head.

Finally, Louis allowed his eyes to meet her's. As her eyes locked with his own, he could've sworn he was transported back to his six year old Self. Those same piercing grey eyes -that had once looked at him with admiration- bore coldly into his own.

Like strangers.

It didn't sting, more of an ache.

She walked slowly - not without purpose - down the aisle, before coming to a stop before him. He plastered a lazy smirk on his face and held out his hand.

"Pleasure to see you again, Princess." He whispered as she slipped her hand into his gently. She rolled her eyes at him, subtly enough so that only he would notice, before turning to face the priest.

"I would say it's nice to see you too, but then

I would be lying." She spat at him, keeping her voice low so- once again- only he could hear her.

His smirk twisted into a scowl as the Priest began to speak. He seemed to drone on forever until finally it came to the main event.

The rings were presented as Louis took one, holding Aven's hand in his own. Her gaze was set on him, dripping with contempt as he placed the ring on her finger, and he hated her for Depriving him of the love h

It wasn't as though he wanted this any more than she did?

Aven placed the ring on Louis' finger before they held each other's hands. Their fingers interlocked Avens grip was loose like she didn't want to be there -which he knew she didn't, but in all fairness neither did he- as they held hand Louis was close enough to feel the anger rolling off of her in waves.

"Princess Aven Laila Benedict, do you take Prince Louis von Lothbrok in holy matrimony?" The priest stared expectantly at Aven as she drew her eyes off him and back to Louis.

"I do"

Two simple words.

Words with so much meaning.

Words meant to be uttered by those in love.

Words not made for them.

"And Prince Louis do you take Princess Aven in holy matrimony?" The priest turned to Louis, the priest's white hair- combed back into a ponytail- was threatening to escape. It was distracting. His wrinkled hands bore many rings and were clasped against his stomach.

"I do." Louis turned back to face Aven, who looked worryingly like she wanted to murder him. He didn't blame her, the feeling was very much reciprocated. This was not the feeling they were supposed to be sharing on their wedding day.

"Congratulations. I now pronounce thee husband and wife. You may seal this union" The priest gave a somber smile and Louis placed a hand on Aven's chin as he leaned towards her.

"For the kingdom and for peace, Princess."

His smirk had returned -as alive and biting as ever- as he backed away from her ear to look at her, before leaning down and brushing his lips against hers. The room erupted into cheers and applause and Aven and Louis pulled away from one another. The pair joined hands and turned towards their people.

The castle in which they were married held a vast ballroom, which had been specificaly decorated for the event.

The guests bustled into the ballroom as the orchestra spiked up with lively music. Smiles and laughter filled the room, it was truly the first glimpse of joy the kingdom had seen in a while. Both in a while, and for a moment it felt as though all would be alright. In that sense, the wedding had already started to provide the hope it had been intended. A glinting array of food, wines and dancing made it undoubtedly the best time the two kingdoms had spent together since the beginning of the war.

Louis and Aven chatted animatedly to some

distant noble relatives of Louis, but neither felt as alive as they made it seem.

The moment they had stepped away from the alter- Louis had snatched his hand back, as if Aven's touch would burn him. They had been allowed a few moments to themselves in a parlour room after the ceremony, but the conversation had done nothing to ease the tension between the newly weds.

"After all these years, I must admit, I never thought I'd get to see those enchanting eyes again." Louis said a bored expression on his face as a light smirk pressed his lips, leaning his back against a table with his arms crossed over his chest.

Aven turned towards him, smoothing out her dress.

"Do not try that smirk on me Louis. It does not work half as well as you think it does. I am not some foolishly adoring village girl. In fact, I'm quite the opposite." As she glared at him, Louis felt his blood boil- ready to erupt.

"It was worth a try. But please don't assume

I'm enjoying this any more than you are, Princess. Contrary to popular belief - I did have a life outside this hellish arrangement, but now you are my wife, and it would do you well to remember that when speaking to me. I do hate being disrespected, and you have a tendency to do just that." He sighed, placing his hand on his temple.

The whole situation wasn't one he was pleased with.

At all.

So he would certainly not be taking any abuse from his wife. She would not make this worse than it had to be. He simply wouldn't allow it.

"And you would do well to remember that I am only your wife as the product of an agreement. Nothing more. If it's not beyond your lack of manners- do try and at least pretend to have least a sliver of respect for me." Aven spat, before she turned- exiting the room. He followed her grabbing her arm as he did so.

"If you so much as dare to turn your back on me again you will face the consequences." His grip tightened around her arm. After a few moments he dropped it with a frustrated sigh. When he next spoke, the lacing of venom in his tone was enough to make even Aven still.

"Let us greet our subjects, dear wife."

After greeting distantly related family members and a seemingly endless flurry of adoring guests- Louis patience had worn thin. He wanted nothing more than to be rid of his new wife, to go drown his sorrows in silence, to rest in his self-pitying rue.

But no.

There was the matter of the first dance first.

Louis placed his hand on the small of Aven's back and guided her towards the dance floor. Her face was set stone-cold now as she looked at him with indifference. It only enraged him more, and she was fully aware of it.

They began to sway and spin, hands clenched together whilst the watchful eyes of the public followed their every sweep. Every brush of his hand against hers sent tingles through his body, but he ignored them.

Aven was not the sweet little girl- the one who would clutch his hand as they ran through the castle- anymore, and he was not her best friend.

She was a stranger.

He was a stranger to the girl that had once been his best friend.

They have become two people who have begine to pass by eachother with relife of not having to talk to one another.They had truned into strangers who do not look one in the eye. and if their past selves were to see it, the sorrow would be deep and endless.

because once they held eachothers hands with emotion and care.

for unlike now. much much more the opposite.

That hurt more than any tingle in his hands. They were acquantences who shared a common dislike for one another, but he was certain they were both putting the good of their kingdoms first, and for that he admired her, and her- him.

He leaned to whisper in her ear, and she turned

her head away.

"Smile Princess, the people are watching."

"I do not want to smile. I'm not happy so why should I have to pretend I am?" She looked up at him - her hands resting on his shoulders. Her anger had dissipated somewhat and the exhaustion was wearing through on her face.

"I understand you're unhappy, but I'm afraid I can do nothing. This is for the greater good, Aven" Her named rolled off his tongue easily, and though his expression was still cold- his eyes softened slightly.

Maybe they could find a common ground? Maybe hate each other a little less/ldot for the good of the kingdom of course. Aven sighed, and he spun her around to finish the dance.

"For the kingdom." She muttered, as she spun away.

The party was slowly but surely ending.

Guests filtered out of the doors and headed toward their carriages. The orchestra played its final song, and the food and drink were long gone.

Exhausted and irritated- Aven and Louis said their goodbyes, thanking them graciously for coming- as they knew they had to.

After what felt like far too long, the ballroom was empty, save for the servants hurrying to tidy it. Louis left the castle without another word, to stand in the snowy garden.

The plants were all dead (or getting there, if not) due the horrendous winter curse that he had been set upon their kingdom.

Eternal winter.

The curse had started a few years into the war, seemingly without reason.

He watched as the sun faded lower into the sky, stripping the castle of whatever glow it still clung onto. Though perhaps the scenery should be calming- his mind was far too crowded with troubling thoughts.

He imagined himself still basking in the sun-light with Kali, imagined her smiling softly at him as the sun lit up her face. The glow disappeared as quickly as it came as the loud thud of the door behind him tore him from his daydream.

"I suppose we should, can't have you die on the night of your wedding." He extended a hand to her as they entered the carriage. There was a shift in the way she was talking, but what it was- he couldn't place.

It seemed almost as though she was trying to come to terms with everything. Paying Louis some kindness, maybe. They were after all, in the same boat. Neither would let the boat capsize,

and neither would let the other drown.

They entered the carriage, just to sit in silence. Both sat consumed by their own thoughts, watching the snowy surroundings pass them by.

Chapter 2

Not Quite Nothing

As the carriage approached the grand castle along the snowy cobble path, the atmosphere was cold and bitter, not just because of the weather.

Louis was resentful towards Princess Aven, he blamed her for the separation of him and Kali, although deep down he knew she had as much choice in the matter as he did.

In fact, she disliked the idea as much, if not more than he did. She had expressed this many times in his company and he was almost certain that she had expressed this outwith his company. As the carriage carried on towards the castle gates, not a word was shared between the newly-wed couple, the tension so thick in the air you could cut it with a knife.

As they sat patiently waiting on the gates to welcome them into the castle, they were left to contemplate the series of life-changing events that had taken place only hours before. All that was running through Avens head was her new name. "Aven Laila Von Lothbrok." She thought of how strange and different that sounded, and if she would ever get used to being a married woman.

She sighed disapprovingly, Louis looked at her briefly and then looked back in to the distance.

Aven Von Lothbrok.

Aven Von Lothbrok.

then let out a sigh that was a bit too loud this time.

Louis glared at her. "What is your problem?" He asked accusingly.

"Nothing, just that my life just ended at twenty-two. Before I've been able to do anything, no chance to attend to my duties, the only time I get to leave my kingdom is to get married and it is for a marriage I never agreed to in the first place!" She stared at him with fury in her eyes but she wasn't just angry, she was sad. Not just for herself but him too.

"You think I asked for any of this to happen? I lost the only woman I've ever loved for someone I've not spoken to since I was six, and don't know or care about!" He yelled back at her.

Neither of them said anything after that, they

just sat uncomfortably in silence. Just then the gates opened and the carriage advanced towards the castle doors.

Louis sat, shifting uncomfortably on the leather of the carriage seat, both his and Avens eyes glued to the floor.

He was wondering who would cave in and look at the other first. Louis kept his head down but lifted his eyes just enough to see her face. He could see that she was crying, as a single tear fell from her rosy cheek and landed on the elegant embroidered skirt of the dress she had just married him in. His gaze softened as his eyes explored her her face. Without realising that he was staring, she lifted her head and stared solemnly out of the window, watching the snowy landscapes pass her by. He watched as the light bounced off of her silky white hair. It was quite mesmerising. His eyes fell on her face, her complexion soft and glassy, her eyes the most enticing grey, and her lips full and the most perfect red. Although he felt no love, no compassion, nothing at all when he looked at her, she was still undeniably beautiful. In different circumstances, he may have even been attracted to her.

The carriage halted at the castle steps. Louis finally lifted his head and as he did, so did Aven. Their gaze met and they looked sympathetically in to one another's eyes, Louis offered Aven a weak and rather pathetic smile, she returned it.

The footman clambered down from the top of the carriage and opened the door allowing Louis to exit the carriage, he did so with grace. After he found his feet firmly on the ground he offered Aven his hand to assist her.

She smiled for a second. "I'll manage." She said softly before tastefully stepping onto the cobble path. Aven realised that she had perhaps upset Louis as his smile slightly faded.

"Thank you though." She said, hoping to share her appreciation for his efforts. He rolled his eyes avoiding eye contact.

"It was nothing." He muttered. The couple made their way up the stairs, Aven was slightly intimidated by the impressive building she stood in front of. The castle in her kingdom was truly beautiful but this... This was just phenomenal.

Louis offered his hand to Aven once agin, with some hesitation she took it. He lead her up the steps and just as Louis reached for the Handle he rather arrogantly said.

"My wife will live in my house, but she shall not sleep in my bed. I will get the maid to show you to your room." With a disgusted look, Aven turned her back to Louis.

"Where are you going?" He shouted after her.

"Away from you."

"Why? What have I said to offend you?"

"What have you said? Seriously? I am your wife! Not your property!"

"I said no such thing!"

"You said your wife will not sleep in your bed."

"What of it?"

"I may have your last name, but I most certainly am not yours! I do not belong to you. I may be your wife, but you are my husband. Does

24

that mean I own you? Does that make you mine?"

Louis said nothing to this, he just stared at her blankly.

"You do not love me, but you will respect me as I did you."

"Did?"

"You lost a great deal of my respect when you started treating me like property."

"Well you are my wife in my home!"

"We may share a home, and we may be married, but I will never be your wife! And you shall never be a husband that I am proud to call mine."

With that she turned her back and left. This time he did not attempt to stop her or ask her to stay.

Aven kept walking with the sound of her heels on the cobble path, the sound matching the pounding of her heart in her chest. Louis' words echoed in her mind.

"His wife. His wife?" She scoffed.

"What an arrogant snob, how dare he?" She realised she had been walking so long she had reached the huge lake buried deep in the back of the garden. She sat down on the bed of snowy grass bordering the lake and took off the white heels. She lifted her dress and gently submerged her feet and ankles in to the icy cold, but pleasant water. She then allowed herself to fall back in to the frosty grass, she lay down and gazed up into the sky watching the setting sun and admired the painted sky. The streaks of orange, red, and yellow and in some spots. It even had the most striking pink. She liked the pink the best, it made her feel a sense of peace. As she admired the sky, she became lost in her own thoughts about her marriage to the prince. What did it mean? Why did he hate her so much? But the biggest questions she had was what they were, and what it meant for them and their future, and most importantly the future of the kingdom? All of these thoughts loudly crowded her mind.

What were they?

Far from friends, definitely not lovers, but not quite nothing.

Those were the three thoughts in her mind from the moment she said I do, from the moment she gazed into his eyes for the first time in sixteen years. She realised how easy it was for him to paint a frown across her face.

She wanted to know him.

She hated him but needed to know him.

She was infatuated by him, consumed by his hatred.

But it wasn't his love she craved though as much as she resented him, she still desired his respect.

As she Felt her toes numbing in the freezing water she decided it was time to return to the warmth of the castle. She picked up her shoes, turned around and made her way back towards the Grand castle in the distance.

The castle was a quiet place for the next couple of weeks. Neither of them spoke a word to one another for many, many days. It was fair to say the marriage and gotten off to more than a rocky start, Aven kept to herself, drowning and clearing out her thoughts with things such as reading, writing, painting and long walks in the garden; she would stroll around for hours exploring the deepest and most hidden parts of the castle grounds, whilst the prince would spend his time riding his horse around the fields and practicing fighting with Demiar. If he was really honest with himself it was to stop him being so depressed about the fact that he was married to a stranger while the person he truly yearned for had all the freedom to live and love other people to her hearts desire. Although married, whenever the couple would cross paths they would act like they were simply two strangers passing in the street. As their marriage grew colder, so did the kingdom. There was absolutely no sign of the frost thawing in the castle of the newly weds, or anywhere else.

One fateful day when Louis was on one of his horse rides in the icy wonderland and Aven was on one of her walks deep in thought, Louis lost control over his horse. The horse began wildly galloping and thrashing its head around, Louis tried with all his might to console his horse. However, it was no use. The horse hurtled towards a tree at the opposite end of the garden. As it shot passed the now frozen over lake, it stood up on its hind legs and sent Louis flying off its back. He hit the ground and lay motionless like a sleeping child for a long while. Aven had watched this whole ordeal unfold, she found it rather amusing until he appeared lifeless for longer than she had anticipated. She hastily ran over to his motionless body.

As she crouched next to him, she waited for him to respond, she felt extreme panic. She hated him but she definitely didn't want him to die. He opened his eyes and tried to sit up but he grunted as his attempt was unsuccessful.

"Careful, I thought we'd lost you there." Aven said whilst turning him on to his back and cradling his head, placing it gently on her knees. He stared up at Aven, looking at her in a way that didn't make her want to hit him.

"Aw, so you do care. Who would have thought?" Louis said smugly.

"No, but if you die then I have to plan your funeral, and that's a lot of effort." She replied with snark.

Louis scoffed. Aven had never seen him be vulnerable like this. It made her feel weird, but not exactly in a bad way.

"Can you sit up?" she asked, but sounded like she didn't believe he was really injured. Louis tried but lay back down.

"I think I need a minute."

"Are you okay?" She said, sounding slightly more genuine this time.

"Yes, just got the wind knocked out of me."

"Oh, well you'll live." Louis scoffed.

"Yes, I guess so. I must look like an idiot."

"Only a little Bit of an idiot" Aven had to bite her lip to stop a grin from covering her face. Louis laughed, the sound was like hearing a new song and she instantly knew this particular song would become her favorite. Aven had never cared to look that closely at him, but when she did, she found that he wasnt horrible to look at. His brown hair, fluffy and silky, his striking bone structure, his jawline sharp, and oh those eyes, she could gaze into those eyes all day. They were warm like a fire on a winters day, and the streaks of gold were like the leaves on a forest floor on a crisp autumn day. Aven loved to look at peoples eyes. She believed that they are the portals to peoples mind, and showed you who they really were despite the person they wanted you to think they are.

"What are you staring at?"

Aven hadn't realised how long she had been gazing at the man that she supposedly resented.

"Nothing. Do you think you can stand?" Aven quirked her brow when Louis sprung to his feet.

"Clearly injured aren't we?"

Louis rolled his eyes.

"I'm still waiting on my apology." Louis looked down at her expectantly.

"Apology?" Aven scoffed, fury an disbelief painted her face.

"Yes, for your outburst the other week."

"Because I'm the problem here?"

"Yes, who else would be causing a problem"

"I really hate you!"

"Okay? Same to you, if I had to have an arranged marriage they could have at least chosen someone slightly tolerable."

"I would have rather married a dog, at least then it wouldn't talk." Aven stood, smoothing out her dress and rolling her yes at louis.

"All you ever do is complain!"

"No wonder, you are insufferable."

"I wish you fell off a horse and died!"

With that Aven shoved him to the ground.

"I hate you and I shall never forgive you!"

And once again she stormed off.

This cycle continued for many weeks; they would argue, then go extended periods of time acting like strangers to one another, having a slight breakthrough, then the cycle would restart. It was like taking one step forward and three steps back until three months into their marriage. One evening Louis was sat on a bench reading a novel, when to his surprise, Aven sat at the other end of the bench. He looked at her, not disapprovingly but he definitely wasn't happy to see her, he closed his book.

"Can I help you with anything?" He asked, sounding suspiciously genuine.

"I was just thinking we may not have to be fond of one another, but we should at least be able to co-exist."

Aven looked at him with hope in her eyes.

"Okay, we may be able to compromise."

They both smiled the sat in silence for a moment.

"Can I ask you something?" Aven asked.

"That depends on the question..."

Aven thought about wether or not to ask her question.

"What was it like to be in love? With Kali, I mean."

"Not what I was expecting but, falling in love changed my life, in the most magical way possible. I no longer valued other peoples opinions over my own, she made me feel invincible. She taught me that I am worthy of love. I took a risk and decided to believe her. She taught me I am beautiful, even with messy hair, and bad breath in the morning, she would look me in the eye every day and remind me that I am loved. The tenderness of her love changed the way I see myself and the world. For that, I am so grateful."

Aven looked at him. She felt her eyes welling with tears and her heart heavy in her chest. She chocked back her tears. She felt guilty that she had deprived him of being with someone he felt that way towards. Aven hoped that she could some day feel that safe with another person, not that she even beleived in love though.

Three thoughts ran through her mind not for the first time that day.

Possibly friends? Probably not lovers, but certainly not nothing.

The two of them sat and watched the sun go down in a peaceful silence. These two people came together to bring peace to kingdoms, and in doing

this lost all the peace in their own lives. Aven
thought that this could potentially be the start of
that peace being restored.

J

Chapter 3

Dreaming of The Past

Prince Louis was perched on the roof top of the castle. The sky unusually dark for that time; a dull grey, covered in a blanket of thick black clouds. The snow had stopped falling for the first time in a while, usually the nights carired worse weather than the days.

He always ended up there when he struggled to keep control of his thoughts. His brain was buzzing, full of confusion and stress, so he came to the one place that always calmed him down.

His peace and quiet was very short-lived, he was swiftly interrupted by the last person he wanted to see.

"Hello, your Highness." Aven shouted, clambering onto the rooftop.

"Hello to you too, Aven." Louis replied, frustration in his voice. "Isn't it enough we share a kingdom? Now you decide to share my spot as well."

"Oh, my apologies, did I bother your peace?" She asked mockingly.

"In fact, yes you did." He snapped back, his

voice light.

All was still for a brief moment, one that lasted the length of an eternity, then she sat down beside him quietly. There was no noise at all, nothing but the sound of their breathing, falling into a calming rythym.

"Are you afraid of love?" She asked gently. He looked up at her, taken aback by the sudden question. It had come out of nowhere, he never expected to hear her say anything like that, least of all to him. Aven had shocked herself with the question too, looking slightly startled as the words tumbled out of her mouth.

"Why do you ask?" He inquired.

"No reason, I just wanted to know." Aven replied, gazing off into the distance.

"Not really, " the prince answered, looking ahead, "perhaps I'm afraid of not being loved again." He said quietly, too quietly, hoping that Aven didn't hear him. She had clearly caught him at a bad time as he was not in the mood to bicker with her.

"Oh, I thought you would be chilled to the bone thinking about love, considering you're such a big gollumpus." She teased, a futile attempt to lighten the mood. She hated the prince to her core, yes, but still, seeing him this sullen made her feel ... strange. It was just not right.

"What the hell does gollumpus mean?" He looked at her incredulously.

"Well, your Highness." Aven smiled. "For your information, a gollumpus is a large, clumsy and annoying boy, rather like you."

"I'm none of those." He responded indignantly, rolling his mud brown eyes.

"Are you sure about that?" Aven mocked, grinning at him.

"Very." He retorted, a small smirk appearing on his face.

"If you say so." Aven quipped.

"Anyways, let's talk about you instead." Louis responded, feigning seriousness.

"Talk about what?"

"Why are you so afraid of love?" Louis asked

Aven, surveying her with intense curiosity, steering the conversation away from him.

"I'm not afraid of love." She huffed. Aven paused, looking ahead into the grey abyss. Her voice dropped, barely a whisper, and she spoke again. "I just- I just never had the time for it, I guess." She shrugged.

It sounded so pathetic, never being in love. How could she go so long without ever yearning for love, for someone to understand her soul on the deepest levels?

"That must be torture." Louis said gently. It was. "So you've never been in love? Like ever?"

She stayed quiet. The air between them was thick, unspoken words floating heavily in the dewy air around them.

"My parents. . . " She began, avoiding eye contact, her eyes boaring a hole into the ground.

"I remember." He said quietly, offering her a sympathetic look.

He remembered it all too well. The days she would protest about going home after they had school, the days she would grab his hand and beg him to let her stay at his. The days she would clutch his hand when they walked to her house after spending a day at his. He remebered the fear in her eyes. The tears in them when she talked about it.

She looked up at him. Then looked back just as quick. He was the last person who she wanted pity from.

"Well they always argued, so it's for the best. That's what my mother always says to me at least." She muttered.

"But how do you truly feel about it, Aven?" Louis queried after a brief pause.

"That is how I feel." She snapped, a little louder than she expected, catching herself off guard. "I don't enjoy it, it's just who I am."

He glared at her, like he knew she was lying. Of course he did.

"I don't know, OK?" She blurted. "you're right! I haven't had my first love. I don't know what it feels like, and I can't get it to make any

42

sense. Love doesn't make sense."

"Well that explains why you're always so moody." He mused, trying to cheer her up and failing miserably.

"Seriously? I just opened up to you, and all you can come up with is a dig at my mood?" She bristled angrily.

They both sat on the edge of the rooftop, not talking to each other. The tension in the air was thick, like a crushing weight on their shoulders. The sudden silence that engulfed their interaction led Louis' mind into a trance, falling into a daydream from a time long ago...

It was autumn but the trees were covered in snow.

The sky was lighter now, but the dark clouds still remained over the skies of Caligo.

A rather nice day compared to some of the pitch black days they faced in the past.

I reminded him of being with Kali, how they sat with a basket of golden bread and round lava buns covered in honey, a large blanket laid on the

43

icy green floors. Beside them a small fire was crackling, radiating warmth and emitting a gentle golden glow.

He thought back to how they told each other they loved one another; shallow, empty promises that meant the whole world back then.

How they walked through the forest, enchanted by it's ethereal beauty, wandering for miles until they found the perfect spot for the picnic.

Louis wondered how she felt, if she missed him until her heart ached and threatened to burst out of her chest, like him. If she beheld the moon and hoped that he was looking at it too. The emptiness threatened to consume him, nearly splitting him in two, his mind in complete disarray as he begged the universe to bring her back.

Then, just as quickly as he had slipped into it, he snapped out of his dazed state. He shook his head slightly, rubbing his temples as reality came flooding back in.

Louis stood up cautiously, avoiding attracting Aven's attention in case she snapped at him again.

"Im sorry for bringing that up, because it is obviously a bit of a touchy subject for you." Louis muttered, breaking the silence.

Louis spoke again after a moment of quiet. "Aven."

Her name sounding strange on his tongue, the sound unfamiliar to her. He said it so softly, like if he was too harsh she might shatter completely.

"Yes?" Aven said, not giving him the satisfaction of saying his name just yet.

"I'm very sorry." he mumbled, sadness lacing his voice. "I took it too far, I know shouldn't have. Maybe I am a gollumpus." He smiled. Aven offered him a soft smile in return.

"You're forgiven, for now, gollumpus." She replied sarcastically. Her tone was playful, but Louis could hear the hurt in her voice.

"We better get ready for this meeting before we're late." Louis laughed.

"Oh yeah I think we better." said Aven, jumping up in panic, her eyes wide as saucers.

Louis started laughing; a loud, uncontrollable

laugh, filled with joy. "What are you laughing at?" Exclaimed Aven, her face crinkling in confusion, a ghost of a smile forming on her face.

"I'm laughing at the fact we actually agreed on something for once, Princess."

They shared a short moment of laughter before heading down to attend to ther meeting.

Chapter 4

Speeches and Disagreements

Most marriages begin with celebration, love, and waking up next to each other with a lazy smile. With this pair- however- the marriage was different, it began with the pair standing in the middle of a strategy room glaring at each other.

They had been on such good term mere minutes before, but the air of competition had rivalled them yet again.

"And what will we do with the remaining rations and supplies?" One of the council members asked, leaning on the huge round table in the centre of the room.

"Share it." He said, in a voice that made everyones hair stand on end. His voice was controlled - it oozed power and authority. It was amusing to see him as an actual leader, drastically different from his usual teasing.

"We cannot leave any citizen of Caligo or Anathena starved, therefore, starting tomorrow we will be distributing it it across the lands." He continued, pressing his finger on the map placed at the centre of the round table.

The council followed his gaze to the map, hope buzzing through the air. Something was finally happening, they were full of excitement of what may come.

Well, everyone except Aven.

"I think we should store it." She said, standing tall across from her husband. "If anything were to go wrong, if any of our plans were to fail, sharing them would be a mistake. It's a waste. We must use it only if absolutely necessar-"

"You would rather starve your people?" The Prince interjected, his voice rising.

"I would rather take the safer option."

"The safer option is keeping them alive."

"How can we keep them alive if they we run out of food." She raised her voice. "We must leave some for ourselves too, "

"Thats just being selfish!" He snapped.

"If thats how we must survive then yes, we must be selfish. Survival is inherently selfish, don't deny it."

"We should keep them alive - it's our responsibility." Louis shouted.

"It's not that I'm being selfish, I know you were all so hopeful, but with you wanting to give out all of the rations, there will be starvation on levels we've never seen before. Plus! How can we keep them live if we're dead!?" the princess yellowed, emitting the same amount of authority the prince had.

"Why do you always drag people's hopes and dreams down like this?" Louis snapped, leaning onto the table.

"I'm not dragging people's hopes down I'm just looking out for everyone." She said as she placed her palms on the table and leaning down "Even you."

"I have a responsibility, and so do you! You have to look out for everyone, and make sure they're all okay, " Louis yelled.

"Well, you're not doing a very good job, Your Highness." She said, her voice deadly.

"I think you should be more careful when you talk to me." Louis seethed, his voice low and calm but his eyes darkened. He was furious.

"I'll talk to you any way I want." Aven replied, tilting her head.

Their eyes met, glaring at each other from opposite ends of the table. The anger in their eyes could burn the castle down.

"We don't have time for you two to be fighting. Enough." Silas boomed, his ancient voice echoing across the stone walls.

"Sorry Father." Louis cleared his throat.

"Sorry, sir. . . " She muttered, standing straight again.

"And when we run out of food¿' A council member with purple hair tied into a bun asked. "What happens then?"

The room went silent. They was truly nothing they could do except travel far in search of a miracle.

"We will have to go and search for it." Louis said, as if it settled the matter. "Over the rivers and over the mountains."

"Or by myself." Aven said "As royals, we are

the only ones immune to snow."

"You can't go by yourself."

"I don't think I asked for your permission."
Aven snapped.

"If you wish to die so desperately, then please,
be my guest." Louis replied coolly.

"Why must it be you?" Aven groaned, but the
question didn't need an answer.

"I ask myself that question every day."

"And yet there is no answer." She glared at
him.

"So what is the solution?" The purple-haired
councillor asked carefully

"We will give you a much more survivable and
suitable answer once i've spoken to your princess-
" Louis said eyes still burning onto Avens'

"I apologies for the inconvenience but it seems
that we cannot have a conversation without trying to wring each others necks." Louis said, giving Aven a glance. That was untrue. They had
proved that earlier, and yet it that moment- nothing felt truer.

"The meeting is dismissed, we shall discuss this situation further, perhaps tomorrow?" The Queen of Anathena spoke at last.

They filed out of the room, chattering amongst themselves. The sound of footsteps echoed off the walls, rattling he doors until it was just the two of them left in the room. They paused for a moment, holding each other's gaze, fierce looks on theit faces. Aven turned on her heel and walked towards the door

Louis followed Aven out of the room, a smug smirk plastered across his face. It wasn't even an argument or even a fight, but Louis still felt accomplished, he had bested her in a dispute, ridiculing her in front of many powerful men. But his enjoyment was short-lived, as Aven turned to him and snapped:

"What are you smiling at? I'm not finished with you, I'm still disgusted with you. You're an arrogant, patronising idiot, and I'm sick when I look at you" she cursed, anger flooding out of her.

"What did I do?" Louis asked, throwing his

hands up in surrender.

"What did you do? Seriously? How dense are you?" shouted Aven. "You-you-"

"Hm?" The prince asked, stepping closer "I' what, Princess?"

Aven spun again, practically sprinting to get away from him.

But he was faster.

All of a sudden: he was reminded of playing hide and seek with her at 6.

It was a lovely distraction from the present.

Nothing had ever felt more bittersweet.

Chapter 5

Swept Up

17 years ago ...

They were sprinting through the hallways. They

weren't allowed, but that was part of it's charm.

Disobedience.

Aven ran, clutching Daisy's hand as they fleeted through hallway after hallway searching for the boys. They didn't listen as Max told them to stop, nor to their own heads warning them of the trouble it would result in later. No. When the kids played all together- was the only time when they were truly free.

Aven knew she was going to rule. Even at 6, it had been drilled into her with an intensity that made it impossible to forget. She would help the people of their kingdom with food, supplies and morale in the future. Or at least try to.

Aven, Louis, Daisy and Demiar grew closer through their years of sheltered childhoods- and bonding on their lack of bonds elsewhere. While they lived in two separate kingdoms, they studied together often, and rejoiced at every mention of trade deals for it meant a reunion.

Daisy and Aven were close from birth. Having grown up alongside each other- it would've been strange any other way. Louis and Demiar got close too, every tactic meeting or shooting range practice. They grew to love the things that they would someday hate.

Daisy skipped down the hallway, overtaking Aven in their hunt for Louis, when she got distracted by a whiff of sweetness. She always had had a sweet tooth, and would happily sneak in to the grand kitchen in the palace. the cooks would lay out the baked goods on a tray, in plain view of the children's watchful eyes. Grabbing a few on their way past, they giggled as they sprinted away- pastries in hand.

"Won't they catch us, Aven?"

"Never! They're all slowpokes."

* * *

The sun shone down on the garden, shining in miraculous rays of rainbows over their happy faces. Louis and Demiar loved the palace garden. In particular- the pond.

It was clear blue, almost grey. Louis often thought of it's resemblance to Aven's eyes, but never mentioned it.

Demiar threw yet another pebble into the pond, watching it bounce. Once. Twice. He crossed his fingers, but then watched it sink sadly. Yet another competition lost to Louis. They were tryin to see who could throw pebbles further whilst Aven and Daisy watched with keen encouragement.

"Demiar you lose every time! I can throw better you, you know that." Louis taunted as he chuckled.

"I'll beat you one day!" Demiar had said while throwing a stone with equal parts determination and frustration.

* * *

By the time Aven was about 6 or 7 she had stopped seeing Damair and Louis. They stopped coming round for play dates, she was hurt at first, but grew numb to it after a while.

She was busy being taught how to be a lady, and how to rule as a queen. Obviously at the young age she was, it was a difficult task.

"Can I go play dolls, Mother?" Was always met with a no.

"When can Daisy, Demiar and Louis come play rocks at the pond?" Was met with silence.

She was a child.

She wanted to act like a child.

She wanted to stay free, and careless rather than growing up just to be stuck in the castle- learning how to greet people properly, and eat po- litely.

"Mother . . . did you ever wish you weren't royal?"

"Dont be ridiculous Aven, you're lucky to have all this."

She didn't feel lucky. Anything but, in fact. Isolated. Alone. She didn't want a castle or pony riding lessons.

She wanted friends.

And then the war started.

Like a storm, rolling over the hills. To the children- it meant doom. It meant no childhood and it meant death.

Daisy became Aven's Lady in Wait, but it

wasn't the same as it once was. Nothing was. The war- even just the mention of it- ruined everything in it's path, and left nothing untouched. The war ruined.

Gone- was the Aven with selfish motives. Gone- was the Daisy with friends.

Gone.

Everything that had made them them was gone. Swept up with the storm.

Chapter 6

Down The Rabbit Hole

Aven usually found comfort in the paintings that lined the Anathenas walls, but today she convinced herself they were there solely to antagonise her, and she found her gaze set certain on the carpet. Really, though, she knew it wasn't the paintings driving her up the wall, constantly sparking a flame of rage, and making a fool of her every move. The paintings couldn't do that. No, but her husband could. He made her feel things no one had before: a burning sensation. But... not a sensation. She was burning from the inside-out and it was his doing. Every ideal she'd been raised upon had been turned on it's head, and suddenly she wanted control. Wanted power. Wanted strength. Most of all though? She wanted to be alone.

Clenched fists dug her nails into the palm of her hand, it hurt but she didn't notice. She was elsewhere preoccupied. Her pace quickened, as she trod heavily through the South Wing's hall. Fast - but Louis was always a step behind. She stopped, and started- hoping to bore him with her antics, but he seemed nonchalant, if not entertained. So much so, in fact, that he began to hum a merry tune aloud.

She would scrub that sound - though not unpleasant to the naked ear, ruined by it's crafter - as soon as she had the chance. She would be rid of him, as soon as her duties were fulfilled and peace was restored.

She took a sharp right, hoping to lose him as she spun into the library, but he was incessant. Louis footsteps continued, and paused as hers did. Frustrating, and only made more so by his being perfectly in sync. Aven spun around, only to meet with his chest.

He smelled like jasmine, so she held her breath. She loved jasmine, and would not let him ruin it for her.

Pushing him away, she flung herself upon the nearest velvet couch and plucked a book from the colourful pile besides her. She didn't care to read the title, she just wanted him gone.

Either he couldn't take the hint, or took a sadist pleasure in her efforts to rid herself of him.

Louis took a seat besides her, and began to read over her shoulder. His breath brushed her cheek as she scowled at the book.

At her clear annoyance, he assumed an infant-like pout.

"What.." He wiggled his eyebrows, unfairly poised. It made her insides writhe with fury, how little her words hurt him, and how dreadfully his could her. "Do you not simply crave my company? Does it not leave you lonely in my haunt? I have been told on numerous occasions that my presence is intoxicating. Would you not agree? Do I not set off the flurry of butterflies in your stomach?" He smirked, face so close to Aven's it irked her. Or flustered her? Both, most likely.

"You are insufferable!" She cried, turning to face him but misjudging the distance and practically scraping his nose with her own, "Simply horrendous. Just as I had feared. You do not give me butterflies." A slight lie, but the butterflies were stamped upon every time he went and opened his mouth. "Your presence does not intoxicate me, but rather drugs me, and voids me of all happiness! I am lonelier with you than I am without. And by the heavens - I do not crave your company, I crave silence, AND YOU WON'T LEAVE!"

"That is NO way to talk to the future king."

"Oh, my sincere apologies!" Their faces were still close, but the wall of tension was a solid divider. It could've been cut with a knife and she happily would've done so had she had one at hand. Rage simmered like scalding water as she tried her hardest to hold her tongue. Apparently it was not hard enough, for the words that followed were laced with evident sarcasm. "I was not aware that your title held any more meaning than my own. Please forgive me, for I have misspoke."

It was sickening but it was an act, she reminded herself yet again. She was doing this for her kingdom, doing it for her family and furthermore their honour. As she stood, the breath she'd been so desperate for but so fearful to take finally eased it's way into her lungs.

Feigning adoration and dropping into a ridiculously grand curtsy - she made sure to hold his gaze while her arms swept the floor. His ever growing infuriation with her brought her some twisted amusement, but that was all she would ever get from him. His eyes - the colour of bark, she failed not to notice - bore into her own, and it was not with ease that she withdrew to standing.

"You make a mockery of our system. But you will not make a mockery of me. If you are to be my wife-"

The book she had been clutching so certainly to her chest, suddenly made it's way across the few meters that stood between them and slammed into his face. Aven's face flushed red - not so dissimilar to the shade of crimson markin where the hardback book hit Louis' face - at the realisation of what she'd done. She threw a book at the soon to be king, but she would not let him see her regret.

Alice in Wonderland. She could see the title now, it had landed upright.

66

Down the rabbit hole, indeed.

Crossing her arms over her chest - as it felt like all she could do to stop the shaking - she spoke. Quieter, perhaps, but icier than before. His jaw was set, either bracing himself or burning with rage - she couldn't tell.

"I am your wife. You would do well to remember that. I can do everything you can do, control everything you can and I can do it better. I will not become some quivering girl just because you can't handle me. Do what you will, but never try to control me in front of our family again, or rest assured - a book won't be the only thing hurled at your face..."

She graced her fingertips over the chiselled stone paperweight, and her message was clear. It was a funny little thing - carved with intricate drawings of dragons and such. Funny, but heavy. That was all that mattered. Louis' brows furrowed further, and his eyes were alight with glittering malice. She practically relished in it. It was so cold - it burned. Somewhat refreshing, in a warped way.

"I DID NOT UTTER A LIE!" His tone only egged her on and he knew it, "It is true. When I am king and you are queen - I shall be of higher power than you. As my queen, you come in second."

"I am not your queen, just as you are not my king. We simply coexist. Or we will, once you cease acting like a petulant child."

"I am not the one acting like a child! You threw a book at me for heavens sake. However- if I was- would you not like me more? You liked me fine when we were 6, no? I seem to remember your particularly touching declaration that we would "be friends forever, so to speak."

"Perhaps. But I grew up! You should too."
"Pass."

"Naturally." She muttered, bitter. "Well let me know when you do decide to act like the king, you make sure we all that you are."

"You'll be the first to know, Princess."

"I'm positively thrilled." She glowered at him and he glared back. His mouth was agape, practically racing to throw the next retort, but a shrill knock at the door halted them both.

"Enter." Louis said after Aven's silence ensued.

The door swung open, oddly controlled. Behind stood a face Aven had grown to revere with the fondness of a daughter. It was Max, part of the more permanent help, and subsequently one of the very few faces that wasn't just a face in the crowd. It got lonely- the speeches, the sitting around, royal life in general- but Max (as well as Daisy and one or two others) helped keep her right of mind. She was eternally grateful, and made the fact known as often as she could.

Max still thinks that Louis and I are in love, she reminded herself. Stifling an eye roll, she stood and took Louis' outstretched hand. He had initiative, at least, she had to give him that. Max smiled softly, the wrinkles around his eyes creating an ever moving map.

"MAX!" Aven exclaimed, overjoyed, Louis watched her with an odd expression painting his face "I thought you were staying in First! Mother said-"

"I'm well aware of Her Majesty's wishes I made a special request to be transferred alongside you." His accent- that always perplexed her to know end- managed to distract her from the feel of her husbands hand enveloping her own. "Well, I'll be off wouldn't want to interrupt the newly weds." He winked, clearly falling for the ploy but still in causing the ripple affect of a blood-red blush over both Aven and Louis' faces.

The moment the door shut again, she jumped back from his clutch, putting as much distance between them as possible. Though he masked it quickly, Aven was close to certain that a flash of hurt distorted his features for a moment, but it was masked just as quickly.

"Am I really that repulsive to you, Princess?" He whispered, for what she assumed was to avoid more prying ears.

"Yes." A moment passed. "Yes, Your Highness."

He took another step towards her, and her eyes

widened. Aven could practically hear his heart-
beat, and it was a comfort to her that it was as
irregular as her own.

"If you take another step, " Her voice shook,
a stark contrast to her cold stance, "I will not
hesitate to throw another book. Maybe the Bible
next, if Alice in Wonderland wasn't merit enough
for your Royal Highness'. I shall enjoy it too. You
won't! I'll make sure of it. The Bible, followed
swiftly by a paperweight-"

She was rambling, they could both tell. To
her- it was preferable to the awkward silence that
would undoubtedly ensue were she not filling every moment with threats, but to him- considering
her idle chit chit depicted his demise- it was a less
than ideal topic.

"Aven." Her rant finally came to a close, and
she was nearly gasping for breath, meeting his
eyes with tired ones. He had said her name. It
sounded strange, from his mouth- but she reminded
herself that they had grown up as Aven and Louis
to each other. It shouldn't have sounded strange,

but everything around them had changed and they'd had to choice not to comply. No one had called her by her name for what felt like an awfully long time, but perhaps that was just that there was something different about it, coming from him. Either way- it merited her silence. "I have a proposition for you."

"I'm listening, " She bristled, still bitter over being interrupted. "Make it quick though. My book is positively itching with anticipation."

He smiled, a sad one. Her eyes darted around the room, desperate for a spot to rest that weren't his. His brown eyes, brown like bears, and honey and the woods. No! She wouldn't allow herself to think softly of him. His eyes, brown like dirt, boring, even compared to her grey ones. She was okay with lying to herself for once if it meant not admitting to admiring his eyes.

"We won't see each other." Now her interest was peaked. "Excluding dinner, and other duties that require the others presence, and even then- we do anything to avoid it."

"So we.. ignore each other unless we have to?"

"Perfect, Isn't it?" He grinned.

"Weren't you the one unwilling to leave me be?"

"I don't waste my time on people who truly want nothing to do with"

"So many would kill for even a fraction of my presence, but I suppose you're blind to my tremendous charm."

"I suppose so." Aven rolled her eyes.

He waltzed off before either could edge another word in. She spent the following hours staring at the pages of a book. Still, she didn't know what the book spoke of, as her mind was preoccupied elsewhere and she allowed it to wander. The book would wait, it would walk alongside her, but her thoughts were wild, racing. She sprinted to keep up as they continued to fall like a waterfall.

The flood of her brain consisted of matters usually foreign to her.

It started with the matter of hunger. It was constricting- suffocating almost- to imagine starving. She had never known hunger, but the threat loomed so near, so near it was impossible to deny any longer. She dreaded the day the kingdom would starve, but she would do anything in her power- though limited, as she was constantly reminded- to ensure no one from Anathena would see that morbid day.

But then there was the soon to be king- Louis. And she was left counting the hours til the silence would become stranger again. She couldn't decide if she dreaded it, or if a small part of her was hoping he would change his mind in regards to their decided estrangement.

Maybe he was right about one thing, she was lonely without him.

But she was lonely with him too, and that made her fear what the future years would hold.

She didn't want to be lonely forever, but she would do what her kingdom required. To do otherwise, would be failure.

She would not fail.

Chapter 7

Wildred Mountains

The sun rose over the village. The village that was then a shadowy silhouette full of hollow homes and equally hollow people.

The newly wedded princess of Anathena walked quick, as her dress graced behind her. She skitted down the stone floors, her feet padding along the ground as she moved through the halls. She nodded her head curtly in greeting to the guard that stood by the huge oak doors of the dining room.

Her eyes immediately caught on the prince, who was seated on the other side of the table. Head tilted down, a brown curl fell over his eyes. His chocolate brown eyes- that she had such a hard time ignoring - watched his half filled glass with contempt. In any other circumstances- it would've been filled with wine to the brim.

It should've been full.

But it was not.

Now that they did not have enough rations to fill even royals cups full with wine.

If they royals had nothing- the town's folk were surely dire.

His eyes flashed with confusion, mixing in with pain before they went back to their dull and bored look.

"Morning." she murmured, taking her seat on the other end of the table.

The prince looked up at her- surprised by her arrival. "Oh, so now we greet each other I see?"

"All you have to do is say good morning back." She said, staring daggers into his eyes, willing daggers into his eyes. "Is that so hard?"

"Yes." He took a measured sip of his wine, "Actually, it is."

"God, I really don't wish to play your games today, Louis." She grumbled, "Our food is running out. People are starving."

"And you think I haven't realized?" He demanded, spine snapping straight in his seat "I have sent letters East, West, and South in search of help. I have begged without considering my dignity, and yet I have no news to share. Nothing I do is enough, can't you see, Princess?"

Aven stared at him for a second, unsure of

what to do. Unaware of the amount of work he was putting into keeping the people from starving. Unaware of his efforts. Unaware of how hard he was trying. A small part of her disappointed that he did not tell her about his plans.

There was bliss in unawareness, but the line wore thin between awareness and ignorance.

Her eyes set back on her breakfast and her mouth shut. Her thoughts were bursting to come out. After a few silent minutes- Louis sat at the opposite side of the table with the exact same breakfast as his wife. A morbid, lonely breakfast for equally morbid, lonely lovers.

For a full moment everything was silent.

"Today we shall go to the village; make sure everyone has enough food to survive a few more days and smile while doing so." Louis made it clear by his voice that it was an order, no questions asked.

Also clear - was the implication that this task was more than a whim. They had to be certain that the deaths hadn't yet started.

Aven still refused to speak, instead dragging herself out from the table, slamming her fists as she did so.

About an hour later- they stepped outside the palace doors and, while forcefully holding hands, they made their way to the village.

It was an act, she reminded herself, ignore the feel of his hand in your own.

They trailed their way down to the village, the ice blanketing the ground proving to be a challenging obstacle, as Avens feet came flying out from under her.

Louis offered an arm, which she begrudgingly accepted, glaring at him as she linked hers through his.

* * *

Aven didn't say anything as she made her way down the palace steps, she was being extremely cautious not to slip and embarrass herself in front of the Prince yet again. Her arm was still linked around his, and to fall would bring him down with her. As they reached the bottom, she dropped his arm and started into a fitful speedy walk. Aven's legs hit the icy grounds, and she began walking ahead, keenly aware that the prince was just behind her.

Her feet pressed on a rather icy spot over the slippery floors, her body began tilting forward as her feet lost its balance. Aven- who fully prepared to hit the ground- scrunched her eyes closed.

But she never met the floor.

She never got close.

Because of him.

His arms, at least.

Him, through vague association.

But still him.

Her cheeks flushed crimson. Her body was alight, as her cold grey eyes met his warm coffee brown eyes. She removed herself from his arms almost immediately.

She walked ahead, her face still hot.

"A thank you' would be nice, " he muttered, catching up to her.

"Thank you, your highness for all you have

done for us" She mocked. "It's all thanks to you that we're in this situation in the first place."

"Me?" The prince snapped, his eyes going dark.

"Who else's fault would it be?"

"Have your ever considered, that maybe, just maybe, you have a part in this too?" Louis yelled at Aven, waving his hands wildly.

"Excuse me?" Aven responded, shocked.

"You know exactly what I mean."

"Go to hell." Aven snarled.

"Oh don't worry it feels like I'm there, " he glowered. "After all, I am walking around married to you."

"Might I say the feeling is very, very mutual."

"This isn't my fault." he sighed.

"So you're telling me it wasn't you who would steal food from our stocks to go give it to whoever it is that you're meeting dead of the night?"

"How dare you accuse me of theft?" Louis fumed.

"I am not accusing you, your Highness." She

spat the last few words. "I am simply stating the facts."

"You're outrageous!"

"You're not even disagreeing, " she snapped. "Tell me that you have not been taking food from our stocks!" She demanded. "Tell me you don't leave in the middle of the night to meet your lovers!" Aven shouted, her face twisting in fury.

"It is not my fault that you read this out of context." He deadpanned.

"Enlighten me." She snapped.

"Yes, I have been going dead at night. But no, it was not to see my lovers, it was to meet the little kids in the village, the ones who cannot play during the day because it snows too hard." He muttered, just loud enough for her to hear. "So if you want me to stop, be my guest, and go tell the little 5 year old girl, the one who waits for me every night, that I can no longer show up." He moves closer. "Because, Princess, I will not be the one to break that to her."

She was speechless. He walked past her, brushing her shoulder as he passed.

"Hey! I'm not done-" Aven started.

"What more would you possibly have to say, Aven?" he turned to look at her.

The hail soaked their clothes, no longer keeping them warm enough. They hurled painful insults at each other. Each word like a bullet, targeted right at the others chest. Yet it was only done to overcome the pain each of them were feeling.

Their hair was dripping cold, icy water, dripping down their faces, making it hard to tell if either of them had even shed a tear as they yelled at each other. Mindlessly. And yet it hurt. Every thoughtless word hurt. Thoughtless but specially crafted to hurt the other.

"I know a cabin a little walk away. Not too far. We can stay till tomorrow. It's empty, so no one will bother us there. We'll have to get Daisy and Demiar out though, of course. You need to warm up. Don't argue with me on this, okay?" He was stern, but not without softening his tone slightly. For once- she felt no need to argue. She obliged him, as she followed.

When they finally made it to the cabin, the sky was utterly black - not that it was too different from the daytime, since the snow always meant darkness. The cabin was small, but not too small. It was made of wood, a fire on the inside to keep them all nice and warm. There was a two windows at the back and nothing at all in the front except the emblem of Anathena.

Daisy and Demiar showed up an hour later. For reasons unknown to them- royalty could not stray from the palace for more than a night without a guard, so there they were.

Aven decided to keep her promise and remain quiet, even though she had so many questions. Even though she was aware that the prince did not answer her previous question about the missing stock of food.

She wouldn't dare say it aloud, but she feared she would never trust Louis again.

Another hour later, she was warming the fire

when he fell asleep.

On the sofa, of all places.

The plan was to head to the Mill (the only place they hadn't scavenged for supplies) the next day. It was too cold out, according to Louis. But in her eyes- the cold was prefferable to death.

She would go alone.

The cold would have to learn to fear her.

Chapter 8

Longingly, Pityingly and Then Gone

She had never seen anyone sleep before. No one had ever trusted her enough, and vice versa.

But this man.

This foolish, foolish man who is acutely aware of how many books she'd like to throw at his face, and equally aware of her feelings towards him (or lack thereof).

He trusted her, enough to sleep besides her, yet she was about to lie to him again. The strangeness of that thought alone was what kept her intent-hooked, even- on watching the slow but regular rise and fall of his chest.

She wondered if she looked as calm as he did whilst he dozed, clearly perfectly happy with whatever story his brain was painting for him. Besides his breaths- softer than usual- all Aven could hear were both of their heartbeats.

Out of sync.

Of course, for they never seemed to align- be it

thoughts, bodies and apparently heartbeats too.

Her fists curled, before she closed her eyes. For no more than a fraction of a second, no more than a moment- she allowed herself to wonder what it would feel like were she to discard the plan. To sleep by his side, and not dispute for once.

What a sweet moment it was.

And then she fought against the moment, and stood with haste.

No time for distractions.

No time for sleep.

Especially not with arrogant princes like Louis.

Aven could've laughed, for how comical was it that the man she viewed a distraction was the same man that remained her betrothed. She could've laughed, were it not the most dismal truth she'd thought in a long while.

She would finish the journey herself. The way it had always been intended. She would not let herself dream of anything else, for fear of being too weak to continue. The Mill couldn't have been more than a mile away, she could make her return to the cabin by the time the sun started to roll back over the hill.

Aven sighed.

She hated the night. She hated the way it hid what remaining beauty their kingdoms still held together, and hated the way it didn't just highlight the shadows- but rather englulfed everything else til there was nothing but shadows. Her world became a realm of shadows the moment the sun set. A world of obscure, secretive creatures always willing to hide the things one loves to keep it's secrets from slipping. Her world was no longer her own once the sun set, and so she dreaded it with all her being.

It wasn't a matter of being scared, just wary. It was always better to be wary than arrogant, she thought. That thought felt rather pointed towards a certain husband. Regardless of her lack of compassion towards the night, her husband would alwayss come out worse.

She caught herself as her thoughts threatened to spiral into yet another Louis-rant. It troubled her how much she thought of him, so she resolved not to waste another moment doing so.

Stepping outside, the first thing Aven noticed was the incessant chill piercing at her gut. It seeped - in a liquid like fashion - through every nook and cranny of her being, before settling in her bones. It was both consuming and draining simultaneously. It was cold, as was every day in a land of eternal winter.

Her second thought was that of the fog. Harrowing. It hid everything beyond a 20 meter radius, rendering her hunt for the Mill, much more difficult than she'd previously prepared for. She despised the challenge it posed, but she did not despise the fog as she did the night.

There was something whimsical about mist. The fog was free.

Free, yes.

But not happy.

Free, but so free that it's potential is limitless, and it's energy is not - dooming the fogs ability to never quite reach enough. The fog would exhaust itself, and that would exhaust the other fog, and then it will be all alone-

No.

Aven stopped herself again, shaking her head. She would not pity the fog, for the fog didn't care. The fog didn't think, as far as she knew. She didn't need to pity it, but she couldn't help the flurry of thoughts that followed.

If the fog could see her, would it look at her longingly, pityingly and then pushes her out of it's mind? Longingly, pityingly and then gone? The entire topic was futile, yet she entertained it nevertheless. It made for a less lonely walk as she began the trudge into the forest and subsequently into the mist.

She hoped the fog wouldn't pity her, for the world would certainly exist simpler were pity, grief, anger, madness. . . simply not there. Hunger, most of all. Aven was certain that hunger would be the downfall of her people, whether now or in a century.

In that regard, the fog had it easier. As did the

trees, the bricks the build the kingdom, and the river that she was approaching. None would ever be plagued by emotion the way they were. None will know pain, and all will die painless deaths. She envied that. She did not fear death, but she would not spin a lie and declare that she did not fear pain.

In amongst these thoughts-

Thoughts of cold

Of fog

Of pain

She made certain to leave none for him.

The trudge through the forest continued, and she found herself exhausted of thoughts. Rather than peruse trains that would likely lead no where, she rested in the silence.

Silence, besides the damp trudge of her boots against damp ground.

The old horse prints marked her path, and the remnants of the day's sunlight peeking over the horizon - lead the way.

Hitching up her skirts, and balling it into her

fists, she sped up to a jog. Either in anticipation, or fear of the night catching up to her.

She never liked to run.

Detested sport as a whole, with the exception of fencing, but felt that if any time was worthy of such a feat, it was then. She could see the snow starting to disappear as she got further and further from everything she knew. It was enough to spur her on. It was new, and therefore beautiful.

The Mill was closer than before,

So close that Aven could smell the unfamiliar yet always recognisable stench of farms. The farm used to grow food, but nothing grew after the snow started. It's ghost hung low, limp as the bricks had started to crumble and the walls had started to decay. It's the haunt of the hero the farm used to be, and the reminder of what her kingdom had once been.

She loved the farm for what it had once been, but for the same reason she hated it. She hated it for changing, and hated herself for not being able to stop it. Now that she thought about it, that was awfully similar to the situation with Louis.

Loved him until he changed, and then hated him for doing so.

The sun had started to threaten it's complete disappearance, reminding her of the ever-ticking clock. She couldn't have more than 10 minutes until nightfall, and she fully intended to be home before then, before anyone would notice she was gone.

As Aven got closer, she brushed her hand against the now ivy-ruled wall. It was so different to that which of the castle- unkempt, improper.

Ruined.

Swallowing down any morsel of fear, she swung open the door to the Mill- if it was even right to call it a door. The rickety old thing hung free and without purpose, barely clinging on. She handled it gently for fear of tearing it directly from its socket, and subsequently ruining yet another reminder of history.

The first time she'd done that had been the bust of her father. She had claimed innocent, claimed careless footing had been at fault, but in truth- she wanted no reminder of that wretched man in her kingdom. Her Mother's nightly tears stood for enough of that. She had pushed the marble statue down the stairs, and had never regretted it: she greatly preferred being able to leave her chambers without meeting his stone cold eyes from across the hall every morning.

The Mill was different though- it wasn't hers to break.

Aven's eyes grew dismal as she took in the remaining supplies- or lack thereof. A crate of coal, a few stacks of blankets, but close to no food. The heat would do nothing to warm starved corpses. She picked up the coal, practically demanding her to brace her legs so as not to buckle under the sheer weight.

The weight of the crate caught her off guard. It was an effort to stand let alone move the first steps, but she shifted her weight over and over, forward and forward- and the Mill slowly faded further and further into the night. She was she

looked ridiculous- huffing and puffing and hob-
bling along with the grace of an amputated horse-
but she couldn't find it In her to care. For your
kingdom, she told herself, you're doing it for them.

At that moment there, she realised that maybe
she wasn't so different from Louis. After all- everything either of them did was driven by the hurt
of letting down their kingdoms. Both were driven
by love, but in different senses of the world. That
didn't mean she'd tolerate him though. No way.
He was- to her, at least- the living embodiment of
intolerance.

The Mill was further away than not now, just
as the sun began to set. She couldn't help but
feel a little smug for her impeccable timing, but
that was quickly trodden out of focus as the box
weighed her down, til she couldn't distinguish her
legs from lead.

Were her legs not metal all of a sudden- she
could've sprinted. Euphoria flooded her- she could
just picture the look of disappointment on Louis'
face, and it thrilled her. Not that it should, she

knew that.

He would tell her that she shouldn't have gone without him, and she'd make some witty retort as to why she was better suited to the task. He wouldn't know what to say, he'd fluster and blush. She'd grin, she'd win. Aven could see it all so clearly and she couldn't wait-

Then everything crumbled.

Her being, her thoughts... her. It all crumbled as she hit the water. It didn't register until her limps flapped messily, desperately.

Desperate. So so desperate.

In a way she never wanted to be.

Breath left her body, the idea of it following leaving only the craving. It was no longer her own. It belonged the river that engulfed her. The river that robbed her. She hated the river.

Hated it.

Hated it.

Hated it.

It was killing her.

Breathe.

She couldn't.

She couldn't breathe, she was forgetting what to do so was. She was forgetting. The river was making her forget.

Again, Aven reminded herself it was just a river.

All of a sudden she was 5 again. She was swimming in the lake near the palace. With Louis.

Louis.

Had he realised she was missing? She hoped so.

She hoped he wasn't smart enough to leave her to die.

At 5, she'd thought 5 would last forever. It didn't. She could see that now. At 5 there was sunshine, there was swimming and there was Louis. Now there was eternal snow, drowning and no Louis.

No one.

She was all alone.

Drowning.

Blink.

1, 2, 3, 4.

Don't struggle anymore.

2, 3, 4, 1.

Not long now.

Aven was starting to fade now, sinking lower and lower.

She'd lost her footing on the bridge, what awful luck.

She would die the same death the bust of her father did.

Death by clumsy footing.

Gulping, choking, screaming.

She couldn't tell. It was all the same.

There was darkness.

Suddenly the only thing that came to her mind were his eyes. His face. his smile.

Where was he?

Where were arms that hadn't held her since she was six?

Where were the arms she'd longed for ever since?

Gone now.

It was too late now.

Chapter 9

The Lake

It was quiet. Too quiet.

Louis woke to an empty bed. He must've dozed

off. He had gotten too comfortable around Aven. He had believed she wouldn't betray him and run off the first chance she could, but clearly he had been wrong. The immediate panic set in, and his eyes scanned the dark cabin, searching desperately for those cool grey eyes in which so frequently had to stop himself from drowning in.

She wasn't there, she was gone.

Had he done something? How long had she been gone? And where? Where had Aven gone? He got out of bed, hastily throwing on a linen shirt and warm cloak. After grabbing the lantern of the bedside table- he exited the cabin.

Unbraced, he shivered as the cold wind whipped around him like snakes, as he searched frantically for any sign of the direction Aven couldve gone.

He had almost given up, when the damp- almost invisible- footsteps trodden into the dirt caught his eye. He squinted to see them as the darkness crept up on him, and the fog followed- engulfing him. The lantern hardly made a dent in the stretching shadow of midnight, yet he continued

104

forward- not caring for wise decisions for once. He was enraged, and though he'd never admit it- hurt a little. Hurt, that she had chosen to finish the job herself. Hed thought they were getting somewhere, apparently not.

"AVEN!" Louis screamed into the shadowed forest, into the shadows.

What if she was hurt? What if she was dea- no.

He shook his head and trudged onwards, ignoring the chill. Her footsteps were hard to see, but he made sure to check he could still see them every so often.

"This woman will be the death of me." He grumbled, chatting to himself for lack of other distractions available.

He hated to admit it but the thought of Aven hurt. . . panic squeezed his chest and burned, causing his breathing to grow erratic. Aven had more of a hold on him than she would ever know.

He would never tell her.

Never.

The path grew winding, and harder to walk on. He lifted his feet higher, trying and failing to avoid the mud. Still- the only beacon he had, the only suggestion of direction were the faint tracing of hoof prints painting the mud. As he walked, his mind wandered to Daisy and Demiar, who were undoubtedly still sleeping back in the cabin. He hoped he'd be back with Aven, safe and sound, before they were up.

After what couldn't have been more than 10 minutes of walking the path veered left. He watched the trees bend outwards to open onto a small clearing which he then found himself in.

A small mill, and barn lay old and ruined against the moonlight. Glinting with morbid history. Louis broke into a near run towards the barn, cautious and clutching the small dagger that was always held close to his chest. The moonlight truly did light the entire farm up with a creepy glow.

"Aven...?" He spoke quietly, but began to search the barn with a ferocity usually reserved for sports. It became clear very quickly that Aven was not there. He moved to the mill next, so run down that he doubted it could stay standing for any longer than a few months more.

There was a morbid sense of beauty about the desolate farmland, but maybe that beauty was falling apart. It wouldn't be beautiful for much longer. Once it had been filled with life. Filled with laughter and happiness. Now all that remained was the memories of what it used to be.

He sighed.

He felt like he'd done that far too much, but there was no choice in the matter. He had no Aven, and that warranted all the sighs the world could possibly posses.

With the abruptness of the winter air- he shut the torturous thoughts of her lying in a ditch somewhere - alone and hurt - into the darkest corner of his brain, before slamming the mental door with all of his might. He needed to focus to find her, he knew that. And yet he couldn't.

She'd set his mind alight, and nothing seemed to dull the flame. He feared the day it would start to burn him.

He was sat at the foot of a dying tree- hunched over in defeat- when the scream rang out, alarm plaguing the midnight air. As though she'd timed it just to keep him guessing, he stood with haste and listened to what were undoubtedly her cries- shrill and full of panic, it was the scream of a person close to death, getting closer by the second, and subsequently the exact opposite of what he wanted to hear.

The scream was followed by a large splash and then/ldots nothing.

There was nothing.

Just eerie silence, that stretched outwards, like shadows. Louis sprung to his feet, heart pounding as he raced towards the source of the noise.

Towards her.

The river lay to the side of the Mill, and it hit him. How hadn't he thought to check? He had been foolish. So foolish that it could mean her demise. She was going to die and-

No.

She was not going to die.

He would not let her die. He told himself that it was for the sake of kingdom, but a tiny part of him knew his reasons were far less selfless. He was being selfish, but he felt that it was okay- given the circumstances.

"Dammit, Aven!" Any trace of his previously calm demeanour was gone, and all that was left was the panic.

He knew it had to be Aven. In the water, and echoing through the air- but she hadn't yet resurfaced.

He didn't hesitate. The icy water stung as his skin hit the water, but he didn't care. He hardly noticed, for the sting of panic was making him run far quicker. He was far too focused on finding Aven.

He flapped precariously, like a ballerina on the edge of a stage.

An eternity passed.

No, 8 seconds.

Then he had Aven.

It was Aven's wrist. He was certain. He yanked upwards, kicking towards the surface with all his might.

The first breath of air fell foreign, futile in his lungs, but it got easier with the second and third.

He pulled Aven into his lap. His face paled alongside hers, though certainly for different reasons. She was cold. Far too cold. But that wasn't the worst part.

She wasn't breathing.

Louis hands shook as he tried checking her neck a her pulse.

So faint.

It was so faint, he had trouble convincing himself it wasn't his wishful thinking.

"Come on Princess, breathe for me." His voice cracked with emotion, but still no sign of life from the snow-haired girl beneath him.

Was it not enough? What more could he do?! He felt powerless, more so that ever before, and he hated it with all his being. The hatred for that left very little for Aven. He didn't hate her in the moment there- but brushed it off as all his hatred being placed elsewhere.

He shook his head, hazy brown eyes wild- waiting for her to spit out the water.

Strangled splutters erupted from the almost lifeless form under him.

It was possibly the single most wonderful sound he'd ever heard. Not possibly- certainly.

She took another gasping breath, clearly grappling for it in ugly unmeasured burts, and he sighed in his immense relief. With one arm hooked under her neck- supporting her head- the other brushed over her face in soothing strokes.

"You're safe now." He rested his forehead on hers, his panic dulling a little. She shook below him, letting out muffled sobs as he stroked her hair in an effort to calm her down.

Her hair wasn't white like it usually was, it was stormy grey. The kind of grey that you'd take as a sign of an incoming storm. The kind of grey that you run from. The grey of danger.

"I-I thought I was going to d-die/ldots" Her

eyes- glassy- dropped more tears down her tear stained cheeks. She was trembling, from what he assumed was from the cold. Having discarded his cloak before jumping into the icy water- which he was now very glad he'd done- he grabbed it from the ground and placed it round Avens shoulders.

Her sobs subsided- but only partly.Her knees clung to her chest and she held them tightly

"I wouldn't have let that happen." He sat shoulder to shoulder with her, whilst the frost of the winter night swept around them, and the darkness settled in fully.

They sat there silent for a moment. the wind blew icy and cold as ever.

"The last thought I had was of you, you know" Her eyes wouldn't meet his. Hesitant. She didn't want to admit that, that much was clear.

Louis' heart picked up pace at her admission. Turning to face her, his eyes softened a little round the edges. His shoulder brushed against hers before they both stilled in an awkward silence.

"When you wouldn't breathe I- I was terri-

112

fied." He spoke quietly, his voice tender. Something about the events of the past hour, and Aven's admittance to thinking of him, stabbed a strange swelling in his chest.

Strange, but not unpleasant.

He stood abruptly, and holding out an icy hand for her to take.

"Come on, let's get you inside." She slipped her hand into his and stood up- no longer shaking, but pale as ice, with her lips tinted a sickly blue. She discarded his hand as they began slowly walking back to the cabin, the silenice was awkward yet neither made an attempt to break the tension.

After a tense fifteen minutes- they arrived at the cabin. Louis started a fire with the little coal they had left and made a pot of warm tea on the small stove the cabin held. Aven sat cross legged on the floor, besides the fire, with a thick blanket wrapped around her legs, and Louis' cloak around her shoulders. She had dried off pretty easily, but warmth was still a struggle. Louis sat beside her, handing her the rusted metal cup and she tipped him a gentle smile.

"Thank you. For this and well- thank you for saving me" She held the cup close to her lips, letting out a small sigh. "I'm not sorry for running off. I admit it was stupid of me, but I wanted so badly to find the stuff we need for out kingdom. It's the only thing I can do. I don't know what to do! And I didn't want any distractions and I-" She stopped when she saw him smirking at her.

"You think I'm a distraction?" He let out a chuckle as her face turned thunderous. crimson.

"Yes. A very irritating one at that." She rolled her eyes, sipping the tea.

She prayed she would warm up soon. Though she had partially recovered- he could guess that she was exhausted. His suspicions were confirmed when she took a deep breath before yawning. Her eyes were heavier than they had been before, and the low after the adrenaline rush she must've had was hitting.

Louis bit back a smile as he watched her drowsily

hug the blanket tighter around her.

Aven eventually got to the point where she was dozing off- but still sitting up. Louis admired how long she had managed to stay awake, as he himself was beginning to feel drowsy.

He stood, placing his hand beneath her elbow and helping her up. She didn't protest, but as she stood- her legs went from under her. Louis caught her and held her up, as a faint flush yet definite blush crept up her cheeks. Tired grey eyes met his with indignation.

"I can walk to bed perfectly fine on my own, thank you very much." Despite her evident exhaustion- she was still able to make snarky remarks. He admired that. He watched her spin around, and take a hopeful step towards the bed, before her knees buckled and he placed steadying hands round her waist.

"Sure you can, Princess." He smirked. In one swift movement- she was in his arms bridal style. Aven let out a gasp and swatted his arm.

"Louis! I can walk on my own!" She wriggled

around a little, but he shook his head and let out a deep laugh. It infuriated her, but they both knew she'd have a hard time getting there on her own. He walked towards the bed placing her gently on it.

Despite her protests- the moment her head hit the pillow she was out like a light. Louis stalked towards the bed, treading lightly so as not to disturb Aven in her new found peace. It was as though all the troubles she kept locked in her head had melted away, replaced by the comfort and warmth of dreams.

Louis watched the rise and fall of his wife's chest, as he tried to sleep.

He could not.

Thoughts of the breathtaking woman who lay less than three inches from him swirled around his head. Swirled, and spun and thundered.

Maybe they could get along.

Maybe they both cared for each other more than they let on.

Maybe marriage wasn't all that bad if spent

with someone like her.

Maybe they would be okay.

Sleep evaded Louis like Aven did apparently. Mercilessly, incessantly.

Every time his eyes shut- the horrific vision of Aven being dragged under water filled his mind, only this time Louis hadn't managed to save her. He tossed and turned- restless until finally he gave up. The ceiling caught his gaze and held it.

Sleep was futile, anyways. Aven stirred besides him, and he fought the internal battle not to pull her into his chest, and hold her so he could keep her safe. He needed to know she wouldn't get lost again. Against his better judgment- he placed a tired arm over Aven's waist and inched closer to her.

Louis thanked whatever god was supposedly looking out for him- that she hadn't died. If she had...the kingdom would never recover. That's the reason he told himself he panicked, for every other reason felt too selfish to name.

But right then- nestled between his arms, sleep-

117

ing peacefully- was the girl who enraged him, the girl who pushed all his buttons and who loved to test him. The girl who wanted her kingdom's survival more than her own, the girl who had the strongest and most elegant yet twisted mind he'd encountered. He knew then, he was lying to himself. He had not saved her for the kingdom's sake.

The warmth that spread along his body was welcome, followed gracefully by the drowsiness. As his world faded to black, and sleep embraced him like most mothers did- their child, his mind was made up of one thing.

One person.

And that meant he was in big trouble.

Chapter 10

A Scent of Jasmine

Aven turned in bed, since facing the fire grew pointless once it was nothing more than a few sparks on some charcoaled logs.

She felt a spark of air on her neck as she turned. She opened her eyes and lifted her head slightly. To her surprise, and horror, she saw a head of brunette hair practically tangling with her own. Brown, chocolate hair.

The prince was lying next to her, inches away.

"Louis?" Aven whispered, taken aback by his closeness. Terrified of it, even.

Aven eyed the blue cloak- tied around her shoulders from the previous night, as a scent of jasmine hit her. The scent of him.

After a lack of reply from Louis, she went to sit up, but couldn't. Something was lying over her waist- weighing her down. It was his arm, resting gently over her.

As she started to wake up- she remembered the lake. The numbing water that felt like knives all over her body, the pain. It was painful enough to allow Louis to help her. Enough to make her forget Serenum, and focus on the man in front of her. She hoped she'd never know pain like that again.

A few seconds passed, and Aven managed to sit up straight- not without effort.

The fire had gone out. The physical one- that is. Not the one of turmoil that had just sparked within her. Standing up, she headed over to the window, yearning to see the snow, and to remind herself that there was indeed a world outside the stuffy little room that consisted of her and Louis.

"Planning to go for another swim, are we Princess?" His voice startled her as she span around to face him, only to watch him brush the hair from his face with tired hands.

"If you ever mention that wretched night again, I will have you beheaded."

She was grappling at her composure, whilst wrapped in his cloak, her long white hair dripping onto the floor.

"Would you like me to return your cloak? Apologies for the dampness." She took her arm out from

121

the jacket and went to untie the string of the cloak around her neck.

"No, Princess, blue suits you." Louis smirked at her, his voice croaking in the morning way.

He evened out the blanket on the bed, and it hit him quite how little she must've had the previous night. He had balled it all up onto his side without meaning to.

He sat upright on the bed, lifting his head to face Aven. Louis gazed at her, admiring her like a painting. It irked her to no end.

"Stop that." She scowled at him.

"Never."

A knock at the door rung true, freeing them both from the other's all-seeing eyes.

"Hello?" Mama T. They could both hear her voice echo through the cabin, old and knarly as ever.

"One moment, Mrs T." Louis replied, beating Aven to words. It always did feel like a race when it came to him.

"Get up." Aven snapped, not knowing what

else to say and hating the awkward tension that swallowed every silent moment, were she not filling them.

Aven ran down the steps, not sparing Louis another glance.

"Good morning. Sleep well, your Highness?" Mrs T gave a sly smile, as though she knew something they didn't. It perplexed Aven further the more she thought of it.

"As well as one can in a dying kingdom."

Louis joined them after a few more minutes of idle niceties, wearing his frost blue winter jacket. His hands lay buried in his pockets as he took his time down the stairs. It was no fair, Aven told herself, that he always got to play the nonchalant one, whereas she was always seeming flustered, overwhelmed. In reality though- neither were playing, and neither were truly nonchalant around the other.

"Morning Mrs T . . . morning Princess. " A smile. A careless smile as though they hadn't just spent the night laying side by side.

"Kids, I'm going to tell you something you must not repeat to your parents. It is for the kingdom. No other soloution."

Louis and Aven shared a quick glance.

"Serenum still has supplies."

Serenum. The third kingdom. They had all assumed it was freezing like the rest of them but apparently not. They had assumed the journery futile- a waste of precious resources and time. But Mama T did not tell lies. She never had, Aven was sure of that.

Louis face lit up but quickly dropped, when Aven butted in.

"You have known all this time, through all this winter?"

Mama T nodded, gentle.

"Well yes ... but maam I-"

"You knew that we could get supplies and decided not to tell us until now!"

"It's more complicated than you can understand, your Highness, I'm not sure if we can even reach the kingdom. It's extremely dangerous! You will need to go through the Maru forest."

Louis finally spoke up. "We have to go, we have to try."

A door opened behind them, as Daisy and Demiar joined them from behind.

"Morning. Everything alright here? We heard shouting."

Mrs T and Aven both nodded their heads but before Aven could open her mouth she was interrupted -once again -by Louis.

"Serenum still has supplies left."

"We're going to go check, see what we can get."

"Great, we can leave right away!" Daisy grinned, as she buttoned her coat.

As they left the cabin and began the treck into the forest- Demiar eyed Louis' cloak beneath Aven's jacket.

"Isn't that your cloak?"

"Yes. Aven begged me for it." She shot daggers his way, and no more words were spared on the matter.

Daisy and Demair snapped their heads to share a look, before giggling like they had done at 5.

They had a long, long walk ahead.

Chapter 11

A Bunch Of Imbeciles

Spirits had never been lower as they walked onwards and onwards, never seeming to reach the end.

They all knew that in order to reach Serenum they would need to travel the treacherous Maru Forest. Louis' doubts started not long after they left, as Maru Forest was home to many deadly creatures such as; Skilliths, a large bear-like animal with fangs the size of daggers filled with poison. Along with hundreds of Nabs, red wasps that came in swarms of hundreds, they were highly attracted to horses. Like the ones they were currently riding on. They had found the group of horses grazing, not too far from the Mill, and Demiar had convinced them to 'borrow them' as he put it. It had seemed a good idea at the time, but they were all beginning to worry,

As they got closer to the forest, and the snow slowly started to fade away, Louis' doubts about the journey only grew. He wasn't worried for himself, though, he was worried about Aven.

Just as they were about to enter, Louis paused abruptly. The girls in front turned their horses to look at him.

"Are you sure about this Aven? You remember what happened by that lake. I can't risk anything else happening to you." Louis said, looking in to his wife's eyes with deep rooted concern.

"What other choice do we have? I hate this as much as you do." She replied.

Louis looked at Demiar for reassurance. "Me and Demiar will go, you two head back to the kingdom, and we'll go through ourselves."

Aven didn't like that idea, and told Louis it was ridiculous while heading in to the forest. A few minutes passed and nobody had spotted any plants, or even any creatures for hunting. However, they did come across a small group of trolls. The trolls in the Maru Forest were not the same as the ones at home, they had much paler skin and were a bit taller. One of the trolls seemed to recognize Daisy, so that one must've been Mrs T's friend she told them about. Realising this, Daisy got off her white horse and spoke to them.

"What brings you here Daisy? Long time no see!" The troll asked in a deep female voice.

"We're going to Serenum, hoping to find some food because Caligo and Anathena have nearly run out of supplies. Mrs T said we should speak to you." Daisy said, making it obvious that they were in a rush.

"We should get going pretty quickly though, " Demiar added, "We don't exactly want to be going through the forest at nighttime"

"Why on God's green earth would you be going through the forest instead of the mountains? I know Mama T didn't send a bunch of imbeciles to me."

The troll explained that if they went left, they could take a short path out of the forest, head straight and then follow the river and would end up at the other side of Serenum. The downsides to this were that it would take a while longer, and that there would be no plants or animals on the way.

Louis thanked the troll and turned his horse left, expecting everyone to follow him as Daisy clambered back on her horse.

"Absolutely not!" Aven exclaimed, stopping Louis in his tracks. Aven told them that they needed to get everything they could to help the Kingdoms, even if it meant risking their lives. At first, Demiar agreed with her, but that changed when Louis explained that they were the only hope for the kingdoms. So that bringing back a small amount from Serenum was better than coming back empty handed. Daisy agreed with them, so she managed to convince Aven to come with them on the safer route, even though she knew Aven would be bitter about it.

After a while, they encountered the river that the troll had told them about. It didn't look too deep, so they decided they would be able to cross when the time came. Aven and Louis were now in front of Demiar and a sleeping Daisy followed on her trotting horse. Aven suddenly stopped and jumped off of her horse, she had spotted some pink berries. None of them had eaten for hours, due to the fact that the very little resources they were able to bring were swiftly used up.

131

"Are you sure those are safe?" Demiar asked her.

"Sure is definitely an overstatement, but its worth a shot. Is it not? After all we don't even know if Serenum will be kind enough to give us anything."

"I suppose you're right." He said, as he and Louis joined Aven in picking berries.

The berries came in clusters similar to grapes. Louis and Aven reached over for the same cluster, his hand lay gentle on top of hers. They stayed like that for a moment, until Louis quietly apologized, removed his hand and returned to his horse. When they started moving again, it was silent. Not awkward silent. Just silent.

The next morning, Aven and Louis were back in front when they spotted the tell-tale walls of Serenum. It had started to rain, making them both smile. It had been many years since either of them had seen rain.

They slowed down their horses as they approached the guarded gate. The gate was open, but there were two guards at either side. The kingdom itself was rather grey and gloomy, yet the people were bright and cheery, Aven thought, because they had nothing to be sad about. They had enough food to go around, if not more. There were small farms scattered around next to houses with some familiar foods and some that would only have been known to those who lived there. Even though there were so many plants, none of them seemed to have much colour. The kingdom was like a grey abyss compared to the beautiful mountain ranges and forests that surrounded it.

"They look like they've got enough food to spare us some, right?" Aven asked quietly, so the guards ahead wouldn't hear them.

When they reached the gate, a guard against either side blocked the path and held out one of their hands, with large silver axes in the other. They were both wearing the same golden and black sleeveless armour. The one on the left looked Aven up and down.

"Who are you?" He asked sternly.

"The Princess of Anathen and the Prince of Caligo." Aven replied with a matter-of-fact tone, gesturing to Louis who rode to her right.

He looked at his comrade before they both moved back to the side and stood with their axes in one hand and the other hand by their side, they looked like statues.

Cold statues, that looked unlikely to let them in.

M

Chapter 12

Veiled Threats

Silas stormed angrily into Queen Catherine's
boardroom, shoving aside the servants and guards

with a thunderous look on his face. He entered the grand room and saw Catherine sitting on an ornate silver throne, leaning over a pile of official-looking documents.

She stilled when she heard the door open, and without turning to look at him, she spoke.

"Hello Silas." Her voice was like ice, carried across the room in an eerie whisper. "As much as I am delighted to see you, I assume this isn't just a friendly catch-up?"

"Enough niceties. We have a serious situation, " his voice was harsh, reverberating off the walls.

"Enlighten me, " Catherine smiled, but there was no warmth in it. Her eyes were cold and calculating, scanning the large man before her.

"You know exactly what I'm talking about. Now is not the time for your twisted riddles, Catherine." He spat the last word like a curse, a sour look on his face.

"If you are referring to how you and your scheming little prince are trying to sabotage my kingdom, then sadly I do know what you're talking about, " Catherine shot Silas a look of pure poison, her hazel eyes darkening. "All these games, don't you ever get tired of it?"

"How dare you!" bellowed Silas, spittle flying out of his mouth. "I have done no such thing, and the fact you would dare to accuse me of anything is outrageous", he seethed, his voice deadly.

"Oh, forgive me, " she said sarcastically. But considering our history, I don't think it seems that outrageous, do you?"

"Our past has absolutely nothing to do with this." He shot back, his voice quaking with rage.

"So tell me then, what exactly is the nature of this delightful visit?" Catherine began to ask, but was cut off as Silas laughed. A loud, booming laugh; void of any happiness or amusement.

"You really don't know, do you?" Silas asked, his voice still shaking with laughter.

"Know what?" Catherine replied, her brow creasing slightly with confusion.

Silas paced forward until he was mere inches away from her, his face shining from the light of her throne. From this distance, he could see all the intricate details carved into the glimmering white stone. It looked like it had been carved out of pure moonlight.

The queen shivered slightly as he approached, his unwelcome presence filled the air with unease.

"Your pathetic little princess went and nearly got herself killed, and she tried to drag my son down with her." He muttered, his voice a deadly calm.

"Nonsense. If anyone is dragging our children down its your son and his so-called adventures. Dragging my daughter off to who-knows-where in search of myths. If he really wanted to help this kingdom, he would not be traipsing off to dangerous places with the only other rightful heir to our lands." Catherine snapped at Silas, anger creeping slowly into her voice. "If you can no longer control your stupid son then I will have no choice but to call off this alliance. It has caused everybody enough problems, we do not need the blood of a royal on either of our hands."

Silas smirked, a knowing look on his face. It didn't matter how hard Catherine tried to bluff and deceive him, he knew her too well. After years of war and strategy, they could always see each other's next move, anticipating every attack with ease.

"So do it. I dare you. See how the world reacts. Because I promise you, if you call off this alliance, you will have another war on your hands. My people will revolt if you dare to strip them of the one piece of hope they have left. Like it or not, our children are a symbol of peace and hope, and to destroy that would be to destroy the very soul of your people. Are you really willing to do that?" Silas countered, his brown eyes full of calculated fury.

"Your people are so weak that they cannot handle the death of a fake love story?" Catherine said sceptically.

Love seemed pathetic to her, a sham designed to disarm people and leave them vulnerable and alone. She would never allow anyone to leave her in that state ever again, stripped of her power and control. It had cost her too much, her body would be a lifeless grey corpse before she allowed herself to fall for another persons lies.

"Yours are too, you are just too blind to see it. It is not fake to them, to our people, this marriage represents a future no one thought would come."

"Your people really have that little faith that you can give them a future?"

"I am a realist. Surely you are not so naive that you believe your people have complete trust in you?"

"Enough of this. We must focus on the matter at hand. Where is my daughter?" Catherine shouted, her tone impatient. She tossed her ivory hair out of her face, a worried look coming across it.

"She is safe, for now. But it appears they made a journey to another kingdom in a frivolous attempt to save our people. Whilst on this journey, your reckless idiot of a daughter attempted to run off and hoard all the supplies for herself, which led to her wandering off alone and getting hurt."

"They found more supplies? Our people are saved?" Catherine squeaked, childlike excitement flooding her voice.

"No. It would appear it was all for nothing." Sighed Silas wearily, running a hand through his greying hair.

"How did you even find out this information?" She inquired, glaring at him. "You don't seriously expect me to believe that you received a letter or that a messenger happened to find you after witnessing the whole thing?"

"I have eyes all over the realm. I know secrets before they have even been spoken, I have stories from these lands that would turn your hair black. Do not underestimate the reach of my power, Catherine." He said her name like a taunt, and his eyes met hers, begging for a response.

"I do not doubt your power, Silas, " Catherine responded, holding his gaze just as fiercely. "I never have."

"I wouldn't be so sure of that, after all, I can certainly remember a time when you did, and I also remember just how well that went for you. Mess with me ever again, and our past will look like a fairytale compared to what is coming for you."

"Your veiled threats don't frighten me, I am not so easily scared. Besides, we both know we will never allow that to happen again. Threatening the slaughter of my people is not something I take lightly, and whilst I would never do anything to risk my peoples safety again, if you dare to harm my people just know that your whole world will come crumbling out from under you." Retaliated Catherine, a deadly venom seeping into her expression. Silas stayed silent. "We must put aside this petty feud, for now at least, and look at the bigger picture. People are dying, and it is our job to help them. So drop your empty threats and do what your kingdom asks of you, or were all damned."

It was only for a split second, but Catherine

swore she saw him flinch at her words. But as
soon as she had seen it, he was still again. It was
slightly jarring to imagine him flinching, when he
had always been as hard as stone, like a statue
almost.

Silas paused for a moment, letting out a long
sigh. He paced the length of the room before he
finally spoke again, his feet tapping loudly off the
polished marble, echoing off the walls. "I will keep
the peace for now."

"Finall-"

"But, " Silas cut Catherine off. "If your ridiculous daughter starts to unravel further and be-
comes even more unhinged than she already is, if
she drags my son down with her, I will burn this
kingdom to ashes and paint the rubble red with
the blood of your people. And that is a promise."

Catherine could see the fire that was blazing
behind his eyes, the madness that he was trying
so hard to restrain fighting its way free. She said
nothing.

He had always been like that. Full of uncontrollable rage and insanity, his mind almost

constantly hanging on by a mere thread, ready to snap at any given moment. It was the thing that caused Catherine to underestimate him the first time, the way she failed to see past the madman and discover the calculated soldier beneath. It was a deadly trait, one that left devastating effects on the land even years later.

"We must get a hold of our children then. We cannot allow them to continue on this ridiculous quest for supplies that won't benefit our people. I shall summon Aven, and with any luck she will be home by the time dawn breaks. I assume you will be calling Louis home too?" She asked, but the question warranted no response.

She watched as Silas turned wordlessly on his heel and stalked angrily towards the door. He swung the door open violently and stomped out, once again ignoring all the guards and servants in his way. The door slammed behind him, leaving the room shaking, a slight ringing echoing through the palace.

Chapter 13

A Glimpse of Hope

Aven, Daisy, Damiar and Louis found themselves standing in a huge court yard, boxed in by soaring stone walls with gaping battlements in them.

Aven looked around her, and for the first time since she could feel the sun's warmth on her cheek, feeling the summer breeze made her miss those late evening walks when the sun was still proud in the sky. She could feel the sun.

Those mid-afternoon swims when the heat was unbearable and she would jump in to any lake, river or stream in sight just to cool down. All the memories of summer made her feel a small sense of hope, and knowing that there was a chance that summer may not return made her feel a bigger sense of responsibility to make sure her people made it through this treacherous winter. It couldn't last forever, surely.

Could it?

She would do everything she could to end the days of snow. End the years of snow, when there should be sunshine.

Aven turned to Louis.

"We have to find something, anything, it's the only way to save the kingdom and to save ourselves." Louis knew she was right of course, but Louis had never considered the severity of the consequences if no action was taken.

"Of course. And also so our parents don't murder us before we get the chance to help." Aven smiled, "Or we murder each other." Louis chuckled.

"I hate to break up the loving couple but we should start moving." Demiar said, while playfully grabbing Louis's shoulder.

Daisy walked over to Aven and puled her into a tight hug, "We can do this. Don't worry too much." She said reassuringly, pulling away from the hug.

"I know we can, but Demiar is right when he says we need to get moving." The four of them began their journey through Serenum, undetected by the few villagers that strolled through, thanks to their cloaks. They had sworn the guards to secrecy as to their royal status, and so far: they were keeping true to their word. If anyone knew that they were there- the word would spread like wildfire, inevitably finding it's way back to the kingdom's they'd came from. Their parents would hear, and surely send for them.

As they made their way through the castle, Aven was mesmerised by her surroundings. She had never seen anything like it. Not even in their kingdom, before the snow came- though she could hardly remember those days.

As she looked up, she could see the looming turrets with church-like roofs. The trees were frozen- just like their own- but the grass was green and not blue. Actual birds flew over their heads as little butterflies flew past them. There was life.

Aven had never seen so much life at once.

The group continued to navigate their way through the kingdom and time dragged on. So much time and so little progress. All of a sudden Louis shouted in an outburst.

"This is useless! We're not making any progress!

We need to ask for help." Aven glared at him, a biting intensity in her gaze. If looks could kill it was safe to say he would be dead. He would've died a slow, painful death that would consist of a spit-roast.

"We can't give up! We've come too far now, there's still hope." She said.

"What's the point? The kingdom is good as gone, 'cause we don't even know how to stop the eternal winter!" The pair continued to squabble over who was right and what they should do. It was awfully tedious for everyone else around, but they were all too fearful of the royals to put a foot down. All- that was- besides Daisy.

"Be quiet!" Daisy shouted, trying mercilessly to stop the fighting, yet again.

"Listen." She said, keeping calm and trying to grasp their attention.

The couple eventually settled down and listened to what she had to say.

"We are not giving up. We have risked too much and have come too far. But, if the result is that there are no supplies, we are not going to continue to search for something that isn't here, so myself and Demiar will go ahead and see what we can find while you two will try to resolve whatever your issues are."

Louis scoffed. "I don't have an issue." Aven tried to reply but was cut off by Daisy.

"Then we'll stay together. Now cease the arguments before we treat you like the children you're acting like."

"Why do you always have the most impossible expectations for the outcome of every situation?" Louis whisper to Aven, so low that Daisy's watchful ears wouldn't pick it up.

"I'm just trying to have a bit of optimism in a bad time!" She grumbled.

"Yeah? Well optimism never got anyone anywhere!"

"You are such a pretentious pig." She scoffed.

"Id rather be a pretentious pig than constantly in denial of the realities of life. You can't control everything around you! Especially not me, so stop trying¡' H sped up as she spoke, pitch raising too. Aven had to dash forward just to keep up.

"I'm sorry that I don't do everything the way you expect it, not everyone in the world is going to bend over backwards for you, just because you have some fancy name and live an a big fancy castle. You're no better than the rest of us¡'

"I'm not better than a lot of people, but one things for sure: I'm definitely better than you." Louis practically spat.

"You just can't handle that I don't put up with your nonsense like everyone else!"

"Youre lucky I can handle your stinking attitude towards everything!"

He exclaimed. "I wish I could divorce you"

"I wish you would." She replied without thinking. Neither of them said anything after that and they continued walking.

Needless to say, it was not a sated silence.

A shout from ahead caught Louis off guard, and he jumped.

"Scared, are we?" Aven said with a snarky

tone.

"No! Don't be ridiculous!" He protested. She raised her eyebrows at him. Once again they heard shouting, louder this time.

"Oh lord! Daisy, look!" Louis and Aven looked at each other, with the thrilling possibly of finding something running through both their minds. They began to run towards the commotion, racing to beat the other.

"Aven! Aven! Louis!" Another shout came from ahead.

When they finally caught up to Demiar's cries, it was not what they had hoped for. Guards. Not food. And what's worse- guards clutching a letter with the emblem of Caligo. This could not have been good.

A moment later, one of the same guards that had allowed them into the kingdom saluted them, before speaking.

"Prince." He said with a curt nod. "Princess." Louis looked at Aven and she looked back at him.

"I have a message from the king and queen."

The guard added, Aven and Louis nodded alon-mgside each other, having expected as much. The guard proceeded to pull out the two letters the king and queen had written, he handed one to Aven and one to Louis. They took them and gently opened the envelopes, handling them with reverence. Daisy and Demiar looked at each other, intrigued.

"What does it say?" Demiar asked. Louis read aloud:

"My dear son, I am aware that that reckless little princess has involved you in her schemes."

Aven glared at him.

"I see your father is very fond of me." She bristled, mostly bitter over being called 'little'. "Always a pleasure when the in-laws are involved."

Louis brushed this off and continued to read his letter out loud to everyone.

"My understanding of it is that she has manipulated you into helping her in her irrational acts. She gets that from her imbecile of a mother. An informant keeping lookout informed us of your parting, and we sent this letter as soon as we heard." Louis stopped reading.

"He continues to slander you, Aven, and your mother. So I'll skip to the end." He continued to read, skipping to the end as promised. "This irrational behaviour has endangered you and herself. Myself and Queen Catherine do not agree on many things but we both demand that you, my son and her daughter return to the kingdom immediately!"

Louis rolled his eyes and read the last line. "I love you my boy, and I trust you to make sure everyone returns safely."

"I guess we should be on our way.." Demiar said, his voice filled with disappointment. Daisy nodded in agreement.

"Kings orders." the guard said, hoping to convince the rest of the group.

Louis sighed. "I suppose we must get on our way then." He looked sadly at the others, then turned to Aven. "I am truly sorry, I tried. I really wanted to help. I've let the kingdom down.

And worst of all I've let you down, I'm sorry I disappointed you." Aven looked at him. she was grateful that he felt this way, and had actually expressed it.

Gloomily, the guard escorted them back towards the kingdom. Aven hung behind the other three as they walked in front of her, discussing and sharing their disappointment about their failed attempt to save the kingdoms. Louis found it unusual that Aven hadnt protested even slightly. As they made their way home, Aven was determined not to go home empty handed.

As the group pulled out the map, and began to hunch over it- Aven realised she had a least a few minutes before their attention would return to her. This was her chance! Quietly and cautiously (not usually words she could use to describe herself) Aven ducked behind a tree.

Pretty soon the rest of them were ahead of her before in the crossing between kingdoms, gaze still intent on the map. Aven lay still on the cool ground so as not to be seen.

155

She was going to save the kingdom. She had to, even if she had to put her life on the line

It was her or her people.

1 or 2000.

To her- there wasn't even a choice.

CfJ

Chapter 14

A Buffet Of Death

The snow began fading into the background It was colder than when they were in Serenum. The ground was lined with a frosty blanket rather than the usual crunch of white. It was somewhat surreal, as she made her way out of her hiding place and onto the path again.

It has come as a bit of a shock to her. She'd never been very good at hide and seek, nor was she used to being forgotten about -especially since the wedding- so it was surprising that she'd had both the opportunity and the ability to slip off unnoticed.

Every second step she took on the well-trodden path back to Serenum was combined with a rushed glance back, just to be certain she wasn't being trailed. Better cautious than caught. She walked quickly until she could be sure she was out of sight.

She left on a whim, more than anything else. She hated leaving things unfinished.

The gates grew again, every step she took magnifying them more and more- until they loomed over her. How strange, that she had been inside the walls mere hours earlier, but felt now would have to find a different approach. Their entry way was found, used up. Hopeless. Then, she had felt elated. Proud. Now? She stood weakly for the opposite. Strange.

Everything about the wretched day was strange. She was strange too. So unlike herself.

"HALT." The guard to the right of the gate barked, while the other stared straight ahead. "What do you require with the Grand Kingdom Of Serenum?" The other guaffed at him. A loud, boisterous noise that bounced off the locked kingdom's walls.

"Don't be a loony, mate. It's the Princess, innit. What can we do for ya, dah-lin?"

"Let me in."

A pause.

"Please? My kingdom will die otherwise." A pang. She felt guilt for what she was about to do. "You don't want all that childhood blood on your hands, do you?"

They glanced at each other, the only part of their faces visible being the scrunched up eyes-

threaded with worry. She almost felt bad. Almost. Her kingdom had to come first.

She rambled on slightly more, describing the desperate situation in her kingdom sparing no details.

Without these resources . . . her kingdom would die.

She couldnt let that happen, she wouldn't let it happen.

"You can go." The right guard muttered, after a few moments of deliberation.

"Thank you!" She would've hugged him, were he not clad in an extremely noisy array of glinting metal armour. It did it's job. It threatened.

As the large doors swung open, she practically recoiled. Hundreds of faces turned her way, and out of nothing more than instinct- she dropped into a curtsy. What was this? An assembly of sorts? A town meeting?

Two men and a woman stand on stage, in what was undoubtedly royal clothing. Dark hues of purples and reds suggested as much. Their faces were

160

turned to her too- and though that of the youngest on stage was oddly familiar- she introduced herself.

"Princess Aven Laila Benedict. Of Anathena. I come in search of aid."

"Sister!"

Aven's face dropped it's colour, just as the jaws of the village folk did the same.

"Sister . . . ?"

"Wait there. We shall discuss this aid' you speak of after our address."

She nodded, fully happy for the villager's heads to swivel back around and the attention to zero back in on the correct royals.

They finished the address with a flourish. Cheers and compliments arose from all sides of the crowd, and it took a good while for the area to clear completely, but the moment it did- all three royals made their way off the stage and over to her corner.

The youngest boy reached her first. Grey eyes glitter beneath a mop of raven hair. It was in that instant there that he knew who he was. He had the eyes of his father. The eyes of her father too. She turned to face the man who had just appeared behind the boy.

"Hello Father."

"Aven."

"I'm Emanuel¡' Aven gave Emanuel a curt nod.

"Been a while, Your Majesty." Aven looked at the king. At her Father. At the stranger in front of her.

He had left when she was 6. He had left for the divorce and that had changed her more than the war. And now he had a family? She had not known.

She found that she didn't care, however. That hurt more than anything her father had ever said or done. Aven feared she was growing numb.

"I've heard the news about your kingdom." Her father spoke, "Winters during times of sun."

"Its all true, and I'm desperate need of help-"

"I'm aware." His eyes glitter grey, the same as hers. "We will help you. You are my daughter, whether I know you or not. Consider this an apology for my lack of parenting."

Aven nodded- not speaking for fear she would cry. After a deep breath, she let out a shaky thanks, before the king and the prince left. Leaving her alone. All all alone, in a kingdom that wasn't her own.

* * *

They were no more that a 5 minute ride from Caligo now- her husband's kingdom. Her kingdom, soon. She sighed, riding the horse had drained her.

Her father had sent her on her way with a few sacks of fruit on her back, and lent her a horse. It didn't make up for 16 years of lonliness- but it was a good start. She had never fully understood their alliance with Serenum, but it made sense now. It was her Mother's ex- husband. An alliance, but not without it's frost.

As she approached the gate, her heart sank into her stomach. Staring up to the balcony- she spotted her husband scowling down at her. Disappointment was evident, and it stung a little bit. She wouldn't admit that-

Her thoughts were halted by the oddest smell. Horrendous. It took a moment, but she realised it came from her. No- not her- her bag. The bag of food.

She slowed her horse, tying to a tree as she flung the bag off her back and onto the snowed-over floor.

She tore open the bag, before stopping dead in her tracks. The food was a buffet, yes, but no...every piece of fruit in the bag was rotting. A buffet of food no longer consumable. A buffet of death.

Everything died the second she entered the kingdom.

Their kingdom killed.

Chapter 15

The Crisis Below

It was dark, when Louis saw Aven approach
the gate. There were no noises besides her horse's

hooves, nothing but an eerie stillness, as if death himself was lurking around a corner.

He ran down the steps to meet her.

Panic.

The panic was starting.

She didn't know what was happening. Everything was dead. The last remaining fields were blackened and covered in the dusty remnants of people's hope. There were strangled, pained cries far in the distance and Louis retched at the stench that came drifting from the village. It was unmistakably the smell of death, blanketed by the crushing weight of the snow.

"The food died. All of it! I went back to get food but it all died."

"I know. It all died here too. Cursed. The Kingdom's cursed."

Sloping their way up the steps to the palace, keeping their eyes firmly ahead for fear of what they might see, should their eyes stray too far.

Once they reached the refuge of the grand front doors, Louis muttered delicately to Aven.

"Come with me, " he mumbled, his fingertips brushing Aven's shoulder, lingering for a few moments before sharply drawing them away. The doors let out a deafening creak as they opened and the couple trailed the castle, Louis leading Aven down the dimly lit corridors until they reached a worn oak door and entered.

The room was warm, a fire crackling away on the far wall, illuminating the room in a gentle orange glow. There was another door on the opposite wall to the one they had just walked through, presumably leading to a bedroom. There were all manner of paintings and maps lining the walls and in the centre of the room there was a large desk, sprawled with scraps of paper. There was a few chairs scattered around the room, but neither of them sat down.

There was a brief silence, the air between them full of things left unsaid. The silence was promptly shattered as Louis spoke. "Well this isn't quite the circumstances in which I imagined inviting you into my rooms." He gave Aven a smirk, but it came off as more of a grimace.

"Have you lost your mind?" She yelled, giving him a harsh shove, sending him stumbling backwards slightly. "Hundreds of people have died, because of us, and you're cracking jokes? You're even more pig-headed than I thought." She gave him a look of utter disgust.

Louis shook his head and sighed, running his hands frantically through his hair. His face had a look of complete panic and fear that Aven had never seen on him before. It looked alien on his features, distorting them into a warped image of the prince. It seemed wrong for her to be seeing him like that.

She walked past him, staring out of the window to the horrors below. Her stomach twisted and turned as she beheld the fate that had fallen on her people. There were people piled in the streets, scrounging for scraps anywhere, desperate for some form of food. It was terrifying to see how animalistic people became when they had no more options left. These were no longer people, they were monsters, tearing each other apart for a better chance at survival.

"How could this happen?" Aven yelled, fighting back the tears which were stinging her eyes and blurring her vision.

"I don't know." Louis kept repeating, over and over. The three syllables became a cruel mantra, melting into one word, his voice cracking as he became more desperate. His words replicated each other, it was almost as if he could find a solution if he became hopeless enough.

"Think! What did you do?" She urged him, turning her back to the window, the sight was too heartbreaking.

"What makes you think I had anything to do with this? You're the one who ran off to Serenum! Now their food is dead too." Louis yelled back, his eyes wide as he met Aven's fierce gaze, a look of confusion shrouding his features.

"As much as I know you want me to be a simple-minded, simpering idiot, you seem to forget that I am not. I am just as smart as you, smarter even, and you're a fool to forget that. Hide behind your sarcasm and smirks, but I know exactly what you're like. You can't hide from me."

Aven stepped towards him, closing the distance between them and glaring up at him, her icy grey eyes blazing, daring him to cross her.

Louis shuffled his feet, shielding Aven's view of the desk to prevent her for reaching to grab a makeshift weapon. The room was deadly silent as they both anticipated the others next move, the tension so thick it could be cut with a knife.

"You know nothing about me - nothing!" Louis snapped harshly at Aven, his features hardening, his face a portrait of anger and hatred.

Aven laughed - a shrill, piercing laugh that sliced through the air like millions of needles, and Louis winced at the sudden noise.

"I know exactly what you are like. I know you're a spineless, selfish coward; a pathetic fool; and worst of all, a scheming, conniving traitor. I hope you burn in the deepest, most torturous pits of hell." Aven spat at him, her face twisting with rage.

"Youre very quick to force the blame onto me, when I have given up so much just for this ridiculous alliance, all to be stabbed in the back. I knew you would do anything for your people, but I did not think even you would stoop this low, " Louis seethed, his voice quaking with fury. He turned his back on Aven, gesturing wildly at the catastrophe below. "People down there are dying, slowly and painfully, and it is entirely your fault. The fact you even dared to accuse me of that is repulsive, almost as foul as you."

"I would never do anything to risk the safety of my people!" Yelled back Aven.

"You already have!" Screamed Louis, his voice fraught. He grasped Avens wrist firmly, and before she could object, he dragged her across the room and forced her to look out the glass at the disaster unfolding on the ground below them. She stared down, her mouth agape and her face melting into horrified expression, fuelled by shock and disgust.

Aven tried to speak, but it was like something was sat on her throat. She tried desperately, clawing at her brain, urging the words to come out, but none came. All she could manage was a strangled cry, biting her lip to stifle a sob.

"You have sabotaged me, and you're dragging both our lands down with us, you vile, sneaky little witch." His tone was soft, but there was nothing gentle in the way he spoke. His voice was engulfed with rage and disgust, resounding through every syllable.

"So leave! Nothing is stopping you, everything is already ruined, there is no point in any of this anymore." Shrieked Aven, ripping off the slim silver band and chucking it at Louis. The white diamond glinted orange in the dim firelight.

It was true. The world had come crumbling out from underneath them, pulling their tales of fake love down with them. The world had been turned on its side. It had come crashing down in a pile of rubble and ruin, destroying all familiarity and safety that they had held so dear. The

172

cruelty of mortality had crushed their souls and spirits down into a deep pit of helplessness and desperation.

Louis stood still, lifeless even. He was a firm, unmoving presence as Aven unraveled into a state of madness, watching as her eyes grew wilder and crazed, her movements becoming frantic and her breathing getting ragged and shallow as she urged her lungs to keep working. The air was like swallowing a thousand knives, slicing open her throat until she swore she tasted the coppery tang of blood singe her mouth.

But inside, he was losing all control. His defences had been torn down completely by the unexpected disasters that had occurred. His people were dying, and he was slowly inching towards insanity, his brain filled with thoughts, flurrying relentlessly past his vision at a million miles per hour.

Finally, he spoke.

"Do you think I wanted this either?" He shouted, no longer able to keep a leash on the monster that had been clawing at his brain, begging to be unleashed. He released his anger on Aven in a burst of blinding fury, the furniture rattling as he slammed his fist off the ornate oak table. "I didn't ask for any of this, I just wanted to please my people! I had a life for gods sake! I- I was-"

"Was what?" Aven sneered at him, her lip curling, a vicious look on her face.

Louis could barely get out the words, it was the first time he'd ever admitted it to himself either. It was a burden that followed him, lingering in the corners of his life like a dark stain.

"I was in love, " Louis shouted exasperatedly. "Something you are incapable of, Princess." He said the nickname with a hint of disgust lacing his tone, his voice dripping with venom.

Aven looked at him in utter shock, unable to grasp the words to respond. He was right, she didn't know how to love, she barely even knew the meaning of the word. It all seemed so fake and shallow to her, she saw it as a waste of time. Maybe it was, or maybe she was just broken beyond repair, unable to love or be loved. She was a monster, her heart as cold as the ice that had killed her kingdom.

But Aven would not allow him to see that part of her. She would hide behind her wall of sarcasm and cruelty, a pathetic barrier to shield the vulnerability within.

"Youre pathetic; a weak-willed, pathetic imbecile." She said cruelly, her silver eyes sharp and mean. She walked slowly back to the window, her footsteps the only noise that could be heard in the room.

She pointed out the window, gesturing to the crisis below them. It was still pitch black outside, death lurking on the corner of every street, looming over people as they desperately tried to claw their way off of death's doorstep.

"Look at this. I mean really look. Get over your stupid attempts of a fairytale romance and take some responsibility, " Aven said once again, her voice almost bored, like she'd been expecting him to have some kind of earth-shattering excuse.

"Just because you are unable to feel any basic human emotions does not mean I must shut mine off too, and only a fool would do so." Louis responded, his face full of anger, but Aven swore she could see a trace of hurt flash across his eyes.

"I am not a fool. You are merely a simpering idiot who allows his emotions to control everything, and it has cost us thousands of lives."

Maybe he was. Maybe it was all his fault. But there was no time for that now. The rib-crushing weight of Louis' responsibilities was becoming unbearable, it was like something was sat on his chest, constricting his breathing and casting a thick dark fog in his brain.

That fog seemed to follow wherever he went, shrouding the lands in a thick blanket of confusion and uncertainty. That seemed to be everywhere after the war ended, people were still caught in an endless battle between hate and peace, struggling with the newfound unity the kingdoms had gained, especially after so many years turmoil.

It felt like the pair were cursed with that fog,

it would follow them until the edges of eternity, a silent companion, watching patiently as their lives slowly collapsed from underneath them.

Louis was snapped out of the trance he had fallen into as Aven's voice brutally pierced the heavy silence.

"Louis?" She sighed, anger rising in her voice. "Are you seriously ignoring what I'm saying?"

"No, I'm thinking, " Louis snapped. "If you're going to lose your head and go insane on everyone, then one of us needs to think of some kind of strategy to deal with this absolute mess."

He was right, Aven had completely lost all sense, but deservedly so. Everything she had fought so hard to protect them, and she'd given up absolutely everything, just to do right by her people. And it was all for nothing. And now she was left with this deafening ringing in her ears, the depths of devastating nothingness threatening to consume her.

"You and your pathetic ego. Youre not better than me, and you should know that. I could crush you with my little finger if I wanted to, and don't doubt that I would.

"My ego?" Louis shouted. "You are the one who went running off and nearly got yourself killed because you thought you didn't need help."

"I didn't need your help, nor did I ever ask for it." Aven said indignantly.

"You would have died without my help, and you know it."

"Enough of this. I am not going to cater to your deluded view of reality just for the sake of your fragile ego." Aven fumed, turning on her heel to leave.

"Youll be back soon, you can't fix this on your own, you're too weak." Louis yelled, determined to get the last word in.

That was it.

Aven turned on her heel and stormed across the room, her feet barely touching the ground as she flew towards him. She stopped mere inches away from him, and before he could react, her hand struck his face, wiping the smug grin clean off his face.

"I am not weak, " she whispered furiously, leaning in towards his ear. His face was warped into an expression of complete shock as he struggled to register the events that had just occurred.

She turned around and marched her way out of the room, slamming the door behind her. The walls shook and the furniture rattled, the whole palace feeling the wrath of her rage.

Chapter 16

The Painted Sky

The grand doors opened out into the palace garden as Daisy stepped into the fresh air. She wondered around, embracing the cool breeze on her face, before finally deciding to sit on a bench that looked out on to the calm lake.

Daisy thought to herself, she wondered how Aven and Louis were doing after their huge argument, constantly blaming each other for anything and everything. She prayed that some day, there would be a way for them to at least tolerate each other.

"I suppose there is hope for everyone." She muttered under her breath.

She glanced around, looking at the palace and wondering how long the effects of this seemingly never ending winter would last, even after the frost had faded, it was more than just weather. Everyone's lives had completely changed for the worse, and it appeared everyone in the kingdoms were seemingly loosing hope for the future.

As Daisy sat alone, immersed in her thoughts and daydreaming about all the issues that were on going in the Kingdom, the weather was getting worse. Supplies were running out quicker than ever and all the fault of one curse.

The sound of footsteps emerging from the from the palace startled her.

"Dear gosh Demiar! I thought it was some creature, do not frighten me like that again!" She squealed, watching him as he chuckled and sat next to her.

"My apologies Daisy, I had no intentions of scaring you." Daisy looked around to see if anyone else was nearby, she didn't want to embarrass herself by being frightened again.

"Are you not meant to be with Prince Louis sorting out plans about everything going on?" Daisy enquired.

"Well yes, but I wanted to see you about something." He said quietly, trying not to draw too much attention to himself or what he was saying.

Just as the sun set slowly, they admired the painted sky which created a calming atmosphere. As they sat in front of the pond, the colours bounced off the water creating a beautiful reflection. Demiar and Daisy spoke about the ongoing curse harming the Kingdom. Both wondered whether Aven and Louis would be the ones to end the kingdoms suffering. Admiring the scenery surrounding them, enjoying each other's company and getting lost in their conversation. Time flew by for both of them.

While the evening grew progressively darker, Daisy had a thought about Aven and Louis. She knew how to encourage them to connect with each other. She knew she had to share it with Demiar, as her plan involved Louis, and Demiar new him much better than she did.

"Damiar, I'm worried about Aven and Louis. We need to help them be somewhat civil and sort out everything, hopefully without arguing with one another." Daisy uttered, thinking the illest of Aven and Louis, and wishing to do otherwise.

"What if we did something to make them talk?" She told him. "We could set up something, maybe write them fake letters from the other and put them in their rooms, that would surely get a conversation going on between them."

Demiar agreed that Daisy had a good plan, so

184

they both wanted to put it in to action. The sun had gone to sleep and the moonlight shone over the pond as they walked into the palace. They payed no mind to it, they were determined to make sure their plan was successful.

The clock chimed nine o'clock. Daisy and Demiar decided on a location for the plan, after pointing out of the window to where they would set up Aven and Louis to meet.

The took extra special care in making sure that Louis would get there first, so it would look as though it was all his doing.

"I shall go give Louis his letter now. I'll tell him it's from Aven. You do the same with her, alright¿' Demiar spoke softly, whilst Daisy giggled in excitement. She had never done anything like this before, in Daisy's eyes, the plan was extremely mischievous.

He held the letter at arms length, checking it over a final time before they set their plan into motion. It read:

'I'm terribly sorry to have underestimated you,

my dear Louis.

Please meet me in the ballroom at 11 o'clock sharp. Allow me to apologise.'

He feared that they had overdone the niceties-it was supposed to be from Aven after all. However, Daisy assured him that Louis wouldn't notice. He would be far too caught up in the idea of her apologising to him to care for her language.

Louis' letter to Aven was worded similarly, but they made sure to end it with 'Princess' as a tribute to the well-used nickname.

"This is brilliant, Daisy. We must set up the ballroom before they meet!" They quietly walked to the ballroom. As the hour passed, it neared 11.

Everything was set up to perfection- on the table lay a bottle of red wine, candles lit the otherwise dim room and centring the table was an elegant array of flowers. Jasmine, because Daisy knew how much Aven loved those.

Searching for Louis, roaming though the grand palace hallways proved a difficult task for Demiar, due to it's sheer size. Suddenly, out the corner of his eye, Demiar spotted Louis strolling briskly past the throne room, and he took off after him, swinging the doors wide open.

"Louis! I have something for you." He said, urgency in his voice.

"Okay, okay, hold on! Demiar, what's the rush?" Louis asked, slightly taken aback by his friends tone.

"I just think you'll find this to your interest."

"Alright, what seems to be so urgent?"

"I have a letter from your wife."

"Hand it here then." Louis said, while holding an outstretched hand to Demiar.

* * *

11 o'clock came, and both the royals had received their respective letters.

Lights shimmered through the stained glass windows, creating a kaleidoscope of shapes and colours around the room from the moonlight. Louis opened the door and his eyes widened in surprise at the sight that say ahead of him.

"What is all this?" Louis muttered to himself,

before turning at a much softer voice behind him.

"Yes, what is all this Louis?" It was Aven, she had her letter clutched in her hand, and he frowned at it. She didn't notice the gesture, rather preoccupied with the beauty of her surroundings.

"You did all this?" She whispered with a grin. He was unsure of what to say, oddly taken aback by her smile. He wasn't supposed to be the one that made her smile.

"It's quite sweet." She added, still grinning from ear to ear. He froze. Her face transformed into one her never wanted to look away from. He was a snowflake caught on a rooftop all of a sudden.

"Oh really?"

"Really. It's sweet."

"I try." He knew fully well what had happened, and also knew that coming clean would benefit no one. They had intended for him to lie and so he saw no reason why he shouldn't. Humbleness never did anyone any good.

"It's working Damiar!" Daisy squealed while

they inched closer to the door in order to hear them better.

"Shh Daisy, they might hear us." He shushed her as quietly as possible.

Aven and Louis sat in near silence for the following hour. The conversation started at last, they spoke of food, and wine and of friendship, but once they were sure that Daisy and Demiar were done hiding, done listening in, they broke into fits of laughter. How silly of their friends to think they wouldn't know. Louis had instantly clicked, and Aven too shortly after. Aven briefly snapped at Louis over his taking credit, but all tension had quickly subsided to make way for a short talk of politics before bed.

They were both thinking of so much more than politics, but they were both too scared to utter a word not on the topic.

As soon as feelings were involved, the pair could never work a thing out.

Better to play it safe.

Better not to feel.

Chapter 17

Repeating History

Sixteen Years Earlier...

The windows steamed up from the heat of the food cooking on the stovetop, Mrs T glanced up from the busy countertop. Queen Catherine and King Michael got up from the sofa, talking in quite an aggressive manner. She continued cooking their dinner, but couldn't help looking up to, keeping an eye on the couple. Suddenly, the King smashed his fist on the table, making the wine glasses remaining contents sway. The Queen stormed away, yelling as she went.

"We can't keep doing this Micheal!" He followed her, but not very far, he grabbed her wrist and she turned around.

"Where are you going?" She glared at him, shouting.

"Way!" As she pulled her arm back, and continued towards the door.

"There's nowhere to go, you are stuck in this castle with me, wether you like it or not, Catherine." Queen Catherine came to an abrupt halt, turning to face the king once again.

"I am sick of arguing with you, I am sick of living with you, just to be used as a showpiece. My only job is to stand in front of crowds and smile, everyday is the same, and everyday I regret my decision to marry you more and more." She walked closer to King Michael as she said this, her voice cold and cruel.

He became visibly enraged, but not by what she said. It was obvious he agreed, but he would never let her know. He was always in power, he couldn't lose control now. Micheal grabbed the empty wine glass and threw it to the floor, shattering into small shards of glass, watching with blank eyes as the glass scattered across the floor.

Mrs T hurried over to where the queen was, frozen still and staring at her palm, blood dripping to the floor. A shard of the crystal glass had sliced her palm, a scarlet crescent of blood forming rapidly. He took a deep inhale before he continued to lecture his wife as she stood there silently as he berated her.

Mrs T hurried Catherine out of the kitchen,

guiding the queen to the door. She came to a halt, catching a glimpse of the six year old princess, stood in the doorway in her pink nightgown, clutching a teddy bear. Her eyes were wide as saucers, welling up with tears.

Whilst she tried to usher Catherine away, she lost sight of the princess and Aven slipped away, back to her bedroom.

Queen Catherine was on the verge of a breakdown, feeling humiliated and discouraged after the argument, she stumbled through the castle halls clumsily.

Mrs T reached the child's bedroom, but she stopped before she went in. She realised it probably wasnt the best idea for the queen to see her daughter while she was in such a state. Mrs T called for a servant to come and assist the queen, and another to get the king to his bed.

After the queen had left, the troll headed into the bedroom and turned on the light. The room was flooded with a bright light, nearly blinding in contrast the the dim tones she had just been in. After her eyes had adjusted to the bright pink walls, she shivered at the cold night air that circulated the room. She headed towards the bed, seeing the princess completely covered by the thick duvet, only her teddy bear could be seen, poking out from underneath.

"You should get some sleep, " she muttered softly to the girl.

No response.

She could tell the princess was awake, but she clearly didn't want to talk.

Probably because she didn't want Mrs T - or anyone for that matter - to see her cry, but she could tell. She knew from the heavy muffled breathing, hidden by her duvet and the pillow that was damp from her tears.

She tried her best to close the princess' window, wind fighting to come inside, blasting her face with freezing cold blades. Then she tried to shut her heavy wooden door, as quietly as possible, the she headed back down the corridor she came from originally.

On her way to the kings bedroom, she passed the kitchen and saw the half cooked food exactly where she left it, she stopped and watched the broken glass being swept up. Her heart felt heavy, the shards of glass were more than just an accident. It represented the beginning of the end, how their fragile marriage had finally shattered, broke beyond repair.

Once she reached the outside of the king bedroom, she paused. What was she supposed to do now? Was the king even inside? Or was he still drunkenly wandering the castle?

Mrs T hesitantly knocked on the door in front of her, slightly intimidated because of how small she was in comparison. After getting no reply for a few seconds, she knocked again, trying her best to make it sound friendly. Then, after another moment, she heard the handle rattling. The door cracked open, a small sliver, just enough for whoever was on the other side to see who was there.

She looked up. It was the king. He was glaring through the door, making eye contact and then cracking the door slightly further. She could see the fury and rage in his eyes.

He was practically quaking with rage, his face red and eyes crazed, like an animal. He looked insane - then again, maybe he was. His hands shook, gripping the edge of the door so tightly his knuckles were white.

She had never seen him like this before - yes, she had seen the royals fight and argue - but this wasn't just another argument. They had petty squabbles and fall-outs all the time: who to invite to a ball, or when to make a public appearance. This was something more - it was about each other, about their love and their lack of it.

It was deeper than any fight they'd had before, and she had a chilling feeling that they might not be able to resolve it this time.

She gently pushed open the door, and shuffled through the gap, glancing around the room to locate the king. She spots him at his desk, clutching what looked like a quill. Upon further inspection, she noticed a piece of paper lying on the desk.

She inched closer.

"Are you hungry, Your Majesty?" She said sweetly, trying to distract him. Instead of giving her a proper reply, all she got was a small grumble under his breath.

Still inching closer to the desk, she could see that the paper had a line marked signature'. Usually when the king had something something he was with his wife, and preferably sober.

She was now stood directly in front of the desk, she could smell the alcohol on his breath. "Would Your Majesty like me to fetch the queen to accompany you?" She asked curiously.

Suddenly, the chair shuffled back, letting a high pitched squeak as it scraped against the wooden floor.

"No, this is to be free from her. I am just as much stuck in this life as she is, the difference is that I am willing to break a kingdom to get out." Just as he turned his head back to the desk, she realised what the paper was. At the top of the page it said Divorce Agreement.'

The reality of the whole situation came down on Mama T; all the times she had been mistreated, caught in arguments, shouted at, and been a marriage councillor to the King and Queen would be over. It was all she knew, helping the royals, whenever they needed anything, and now it was over? As much as she felt important, like a part of the royal family, she was just a servant. That's all she was and would ever be, no time for a family, no time to make friends. She always thought the royals were the closest thing she had to family. But, in the end, all they thought of her was someone to open doors or make their food. Would it all end? Or was she going to be stuck in another royal couples life next? Would it be the same as this one?

Life couldn't go on like that forever ... could it?

Chapter 18

The Big Reveal

The crunch of their boots hitting the snow echoed throughout the Tatilin forest. They be-

gin to move- the ice melting off the trees going
completely unnoticed by the two royals.

"Why are we going to her?" Louis complained,
sounding every bit the petulant child Aven had
accused him of being, "Why can't she just come
to us?"

"Can you not whine for two minutes, or is that
beyond you too- OW!" A small acorn hit her head,
cutting her off.

"Are you alright?" The prince asked quickly
moving towards her, concern evident on his usually smug face.

She rubbed her head, wincing. His hand moved
over hers, gently patting her white hair only made
whiter by the dusting of snow. She moved her
hand from beneath his, as fast as possible- whilst
her face went impossibly hot. She was certain her
face must match the colour of her crimson dress.

"What's wrong?" He asked again, "Are you
hurt?" His voice sounded so full of genuine worry-
it both irked an flattered her.

"Im fine." She said quietly, her usually pale

face lighting with a blush as she patted the snow from her hair. "Just an acorn-"

"Those darn acorns! I knew they were no good. Want me to chop the tree down for you?" He bristled, looking up at the trees with the rage of a killer. She chuckled lightly.

"Only you find them annoying, leave the poor acorns be." she muttered, still a little flustered, "Come on! Let's get going already."

They begin their journey through the Tatilin forest again. The journey to find Mrs T.

Mrs T- whom they trusted so much. Mrs T who raised them. Mrs T who had been with them since the ripe age of 6.

Mrs T whom they least suspected.

And yet . . .

It was her.

It was always the ones you trust.

It was always the ones you trust the most.

Most people would be foolish, to show up to the kingdom's strongest being's house unarmed. But they were not most people. They were of noble blood, and with that came immunity. With that came power. Nothing affected them. No one could hurt them besides another royal.

Except another royal.

His eyes wandered to a certain grey eyed royal, walking in front of him. Hair as white as the snow falling on her. Cheeks twinged with the flush pink of berries. The way the snow sprinkled her looked so lovely, ever so lovely. It practically glittered. Like fairy dust, like magic. Snow that would burn other's skin looked oh so beatiful on her.

Poison masked with beauty.

Just like her.

Except another royal.

A hut- made messily of wood- came into view just as he began to fear they might of taken a wrong turn. It's windows were made of glass- looking no stronger than bubbles itching to pop. Moss climbed the walls, alongside a painted door- the vibrant red of Musher berries.

It was slanted, perhaps, but looked functional.

Troll's clearly didn't have particularly high living standards.

"You ready, Princess?" He whispered, coming up to stand behind her.

She looked up at him slowly. Every move she made affected him as much as it did her. They were intertwined. Simultaneously the two most different souls, and one combined. Magical.

"Only if you are." She whispered back.

"I'm always up for a little fun." He smiled at her, but she saw through. Through the mask he placed over himself. Through the calm, he was frightened.

"Alright." She said, after staring at him mindlessly for what must have been a while. "Let's do this."

They knocked three times.

The door swung upon, and Mama T grinned up at them, framed by walls of vines and rock.

The smile isn't happy, far from it in fact. It was the same smile she'd given them after passing a test, and the same smile she'd flashed at their wedding day. Perhaps it truly had been ugly all

along, but they were blinded to it's lack of charm
by love.

Most trolls were nothing to the kingdom. Most
were common house servants, or at best: chauf-
feurs. But not Mama T. She was powerful.

She could curse, hex and kill. At every whim
or will. It was power gifted to one who couldn't
deserve it any less.

"Ah! My favourite newlyweds. How may I
help you?" Aven grimaced at the sight of her
sharp teeth- sharpened further into little spikes,
jagged enough to hurt. She wondered if they'd
ever done so, but that was unwise considering they
had to confront her shortly after.

"We needed to know" The prince spoke up,
before correcting himself, "Correction, we had to
find out ourselves. The truth."

"And what may that truth be?" Mrs T asked,
curitosity peaked.

"You did this." Aven said, finally dropping
the act of calm, and instead practically hissing.
"Didn't you? It was you. Wasn't it-"

"Princess." Louis' voice dropped into her ear, a hush, but still a warning. It calmed her just as he'd intended.

"Let us in." She said straightening her back, and assuming a regal posture. "As the princess of this land, I command you to let us in!"

* * *

"Do not tell us that you didn't do as you did." Louis told her, shrill anger seeping into his tone no matter how he tried to restrain it, "We know otherwise."

They sat in a ring of stools, made purely from the wood of the very forest they sat in. Sipping mugs of hot water- Aven and Louis huddled close while distancing themselves from the traitor and regarding Mama T with reproach.

For a moment- there was silence.

"It is not as it seems."

"Is it truly? Not as it seems? It seems perfectly clear to me." Aven snapped, patience wearing thinner by the moment, like a tightrope. It was bound to snap, and the people were bound to fall, but when? A mystery. "Because as far as I know- this kingdom Has been carpeted by snow, growing nothing but Pine and Copter trees. People have starved for 20 years. Your doing, no? Tell me it's not your doing and I'll believe you! I WANT TO TRUST YOU, JUST GIVE ME A REASON TOO!"

"Let me explain myself." Mrs T said slowly. Surely, but there was a trace of fear. Perhaps it was in the speed, if not that then the slight raise in pitch.

"I'd get to it. Stat. My Princess here tends to be a bit/ldots reckless, when it comes to punishing traitors." He leant back into his chair, arms crossed and eyes gleaming with pride as he watched Aven. "She will rip you apart."

"I'm sure she will." Mrs T muttered, an annoyed glance sliding the princess' way.

"Well?" The princess demanded. She was already planning to ruin Mrs T, but Louis' praises were the cherry on top. It shouldn't have been, but it was certainly a sweet note in such a bitter environment.

Mrs T sighed.

"I wanted peace." She said quietly, sad. "I wanted the two kingdoms at peace."

"I have been alive for over 10 decades. I've seen death unlike you children can imagine. I've seen many, many rulers - from both kingdoms - fight and fight. War after war, it seemed never ending."

"As though citizens of each kingdom were only raised for war. Born to fight and to be sliced by the metal blades of war. Born to die. For decades I've seen pain. For decades I have seen how cruel the world could be. Is it really so bad to want to end that?."

"So I thought." She began again, before either of them could speak, "If the kingdoms could not cease the fighting, perhaps starving would be preferable. At least they could anticipate their deaths. At least they'd die together, if the kingdom's couldn't find peace."

"You cursed us/ldots" The prince growled, eyes

turning black as repeated her words back to her, "You cursed us because you couldn't stand war?"

"Louis." Aven put her hand over his.

"I only did it because I had to-"

"You could have spoken to the rulers-"

"And would they have listened?" Mrs T demanded, her grey skin fading the red of her hair, "You know fine well they wouldn't. "

They were silent

"It was not a choice between good and evil." She said quietly "But rather a certain death, or a chance at life. I gave you a chance."

She walked across the room, pulling a blue book from the clutch of the shelf. From it, fell a sheet of parchment- covered in hardly legible scrawls.

"This, was the prophecy. Written by my ancestors." She held the paper with reverance, before hesitantly placing it in the prince's outstretched hand.

"If the prince born to the sun, and the princess born to the night would not be bonded by something greater than friendship, the world would collapse and be left with nothing but blood and anguish."

"You were born dead at the night, " she said, pointing a shrivelled finger at Aven, before turning to Louis and speaking again, more certain this time. "You were born as the birds began to chirp. Or perhaps- the birds began to chirp as you were born. Sunrise, and sunsight. Night and Day."

"What does that have to do-"

"I knew immediately that was is you two the prophecy spoke of." She sighed. "You would not be the lovers you were destined to be, for war would hold you apart. War would ruin you both and leave you do jagged- your spikes would no longer fit. You would collide, but never merge. A failed collision."

"So I did what I must." She whispered, sounding almost sad. "I cursed the kingdom. I set the prophecy into motion. The only way to truly cure the curse was if you two fell in love."

"Greater than friendship." Aven whispered,

repeating the prophecy. Her eyes flashed lightning, a bright light of understanding. They understood.

Louis looked at her. Really looked at her.

He wondered if she knew just how close they'd come to breaking the curse. He had fallen for her, but rather than fall- he had collapsed. He was a heap for her. Every little flaw of hers defined him, but they weren't flaws. They were perfect. Beautiful, dangerous, and fiery. Her.

So close, yet so far.

Half way there, perhaps.

He had collapsed for her,

But she had not fallen for him.

He was fairly sure of that.

"You cannot force two to fall in love, " he snapped, glaring at the troll, face as cold as the ice outside.

Aven didn't dare look at him. Didn't dare do anything that would give her away. She stayed static, still. Frozen.

She looked ahead. Trying desperately to feign

normality. He couldn't know. She wouldn't tell him. She was afraid. Too afraid that he would find out what she had tried so hard to hide. What she did not want to admit. Something that would save her kingdom, but ruin her heart in the process.

Shatter it, into pieces of dust.

Pieces of snow.

Snow.

Beautiful snow.

"I am aware." The troll began. "It was not reasonable, but there was no other solution-"

"Enough of this." Aven got up. "I will not hear another word of your ridiculous reasoning. You had good intentions, and for that I may have praised you. For caring about the creatures of our land, especially when their protectors didn't, I truly do praise you. But that is no excuse to force them to suffer further. It is no reason to force two people who are so indifferent upon each other. There is no reason to starve."

The prince stood too, standing beside her.

"Get rid of it." He barked. "The curse. If you can cast it, then you must be able to get rid of it."

"We will take our leave." That was all that was said, the two royals marching out of the doors With haste.

The troll smiled to herself as they made their way back to the castle gates. They didn't know that they had done it. They didn't yet know that the people wouldn't starve.

They didn't know they were in love.

Chapter 19

Confessions

It had been one day.

A full day since the curse was lifted, and the

kingdom had seemingly gone back to its usual ways.

The snow slowly dried out, and birds flew over the now clear and blue skies. It all seemed to finally be working its way back to normal. The sun kissed the frozen rivers, making them melt under her touch. The crops came back to be harvested. And the war was finally over.

Finally.

And yet, Aven was sitting on the rooftop of the castle, looking over the sky that had gone dark. The stars were there for those who weren't yet asleep. For those who were troubled.

For those who were the Princess of Anathena.

It was the first night in years with a starlit sky. And yet it only comforted a small part of her.

The other remained a certain brunette whose eyes were as warm as a cup of coffee, and a smile that lit up even the darkest of rooms. Unknowingly being the one who comforted her in the coldest and darkest of days.

The other remained inconsolable.

And yet, now that all was well, Louis had probably gone back to his true lover. The one who he truly wanted to be with. Stuck by her side, just like all the times that he had been stuck by Aven's.

Aven had no right to be angry. It wasn't like they were together. She was the one who said they shouldn't be involved romantically, she's the one who said that they should only be together for the good of the people.

She was the one who said she didn't care.

And yet ...

She was sitting there, her mind stuck on his warm smile.

"Hey." A deep voice exhaled from behind her. "I caught you."

She looked up. Louis.

"Hey." She whispered back.

"So, what are you running away from?" He asked, sitting beside her. His long limbs dangled over the edge of the roof top.

You.

"No one."

"Oh, so it's a someone?" He quirked an eyebrow with a smile. There was silence for a second.

"What are you doing here?" She asked, looking at him suspiciously.

"Can I not be here?"

"No- I just-" she breathed. "I just assumed you'd be with Tibet."

"Why in the hell would I be with Demiar?"

"Kali."

"Oh." He whispered. "And why would you assume so?"

"Because she is your true lover." She whispered. "And now that all is over, and Mrs T has taken mercy upon us and undone the curse, I assume our work here is done."

"Ah yes." He said bitterly. "You just couldn't wait to get out of this."

Why was he so angry? It was all over, and now he finally had a chance to be reunited with the girl he loved. Yet he was here, with her. It made no sense. He didn't care about her, and he most definitely did not have the right to be upset with her. So why was he here?

"No, you're getting me- this- all wrong." She stuttered, trying desperately to grasp the words that were caught in the back of her throat. They slipped through like running water through her palms.

"Am I?" He questioned, coldness in his voice. "You were very excited to get all of this over with, I'm sure you were happy for me too . . . considering you wanted to get rid of me the second you found out we had to get married- "

"That's not true!" Aven interrupted, standing up.

"Oh yes it is." He got up too, towering over her- casting the impression that she was still seated, "And you know it, Princess."

"You're the one who was hung over Kali-Ker, and you're the one who got all upset that it wasn't her you married- "

"Why are you so hung up over what I wanted in the past¿'

"Is it not what you want?" She moved closer, suddenly feeling a little hopeful.

He was silent for a moment.

"That's what I thought." She took a step back. She shouldn't have felt it. She should have ignored it.

"Now that everything is fixed, " he began sternly. "And you have nothing to fight with me about, you bring Kali-ker into it - is that it?"

"I would rather talk about moss, " she snapped. "And no, I have plenty to fight about, thank you very much."

"Ah, well then." Louis began, giving her a smirk.

"For example, why are you dressed in last nights clothing? Are you incapable of changing?"

"Why would you care?"

"Because I do-"

"I couldn't sleep, okay?" Louis sighed, running his hands through his hair, shaking his head in exhaustion. Exasperation was heavily mixed in the movement too.

"And isn't that more of a reason for you to get changed out of that wretched clothing?"

"And yet I didn't, and this has nothing to do with you. It is not my fault that you seen uncomfortable with love and would not wish to talk about it."

"I am not uncomfortable with love." She huffed angrily.

"Oh, I'm sure." Louis responded sarcastically, rolling his eyes so far she feared they may get stuck.

"Go away." Aven sighed, frustrated.

"That, I cannot do." Louis grumbled.

"And why is that? I'm sure you find great pleasure in hurting me, and I'm sure you would love to insult me - if that's the last thing you do. But I do not wish to be talking to you. I really don't want to I really can't fight with you right now. And I certainly don't want to be talking about the love of your life. Please consult Demiar if you are desperate to talk about love, or more specifically, Kali." She spat the last part like it was venom."

"You brought that up, " He said as he stepped closer. "I have no intention about taking about her. And she is not the love of my life'." Louis snarled, mocking Avens cruel words.

"I only brought up what was on your mind." Aven retorted sharply.

"Sure, because you know exactly what goes on in my head, I forgot." He yelled back sarcastically.

"I know you better than you think, " She snapped. "I know that you hate pine trees, because the small acorns would fall on you when we went through the woods. I know your favourite colour is black because your mother would always wear that colour, I know you don't eat when youre upset, I know you don't sleep when you have a lot on your mind. And I remember how even after your mother passed, you still stuck by my side when I couldn't bear to hear my parents fight."

She stopped, realising she'd said too much. She looked away when she felt her cheeks heating up, so that he couldn't see her face turning scarlet.

"And I know you just as well." He whispered softly. "Even better, if I do say so." Aven scoffed.

"If you say so." Aven rolled her eyes.

"And I certainly know that's its unlike you to care so much about my past love life, " He began, before being cut off by Aven.

"Since you say you know so much." She mumbled. "I don't believe that you know me, and I certainly don't care at all about your stupid, pointless, immature, outrageous-" Her voice crescendoed into a yell, but was interrupted by Louis.

"Yes?" He cocked his brow, grinning.

She looked upwards to find him looking down at her, much closer than she remembered him being, his face mere inches away. Suddenly she felt so hot.

"No, no, please, go on, I'd love hear what you're about to say, " smirked Louis.

"Relationships." she spat, her voice icy, full of disgust. If he really wanted to know, then he shall, Aven thought.

"Interesting." He murmured. "You talk with such disgust now, and yet before you spoke with such interest."

"Oh, for heavens sake, " She turned, only to be swivelled back.

"We're not done." He growled.

"Fine then." She stepped closer. So close.

So close.

So close, basically breathing his air.

So close, that she could see the gleam in his eyes.

"You want to talk about Kali, lets talk about her." She seethed.

"I don't want to talk about her. I want to talk about you." He growled "I want to talk about us. I want to know how you are today. I want to know if you're okay. I want to know if you ate. I want to know if your mother came to have another word with you. I want to know if youre cold. I want to know if you're hurt. I want to know if you hate me more than you used to. I want to know - I want to know everything about you that I don't already know. I want a lot of things I can't have."

"And why would you care? Why would you want to do any of this-" She yelled out.

"Isn't it obvious?" He growled, his voice so deep and thick, so loud, echoing through the night. "I only want you."

She stared at him, stunned.

The prince regretted the words as they came out. He shouldn't have said them. He shouldn't have, she would run away now. She would walk off and leave him. She would laugh in his face and he would have to bear the humiliation for the rest of his life. Until she found someone she loved. She would make fun of him until that day came.

His glare moved between her stormy eyes. He gulped, trying to come up with something to say that would make her believe otherwise.

"I-"

She pressed her mouth onto his. His lips felt precious.

He freezes taken by surprise by the whole situation.

Her lips on his.

Her hands on his neck.

Her lips on his.

Her lips on his.

Everything was happening so fast, but he certainly wasn't complaining.

He pressed his lips back onto hers, and his hands wrapped around her waist pulling her closer, she felt like she couldnt breath. She couldn't breathe. She didn't need to anymore, his lips were all she needed. He was all she needed.

Her hands went through his hair, gently tugging it.

He forgot to breathe.

Louis tucked a strand of a snowy white hair behind her ear, tilting her head in the process.

Lips pressed against each other, moving as if meant for each other, as if the final piece of a puzzle had finally been pieced together. As if moulded to be in this very position. Ironic how every part of them was against each other but now even their heartbeats sounded the same.

They were both running out of air.

But they couldn't care. Not now.

They would happily suffocate if it meant staying together a moment longer.

"Princess . . . " Louis whispered.

"I'm sorry." She pulled back, taking a slow breath as she did.

He wrapped an arm around her waist, pulling her in closer, leaning his forehead against hers. "Guilty, aren't you." He chuckled

"Shut up and kiss me again." She whispered.

And that he did.

Chapter 20

For Love

It had been a month since snow had carpeted every crevice of the village. It had been a month since the end of the Winter Curse's reign ended. A month of sunshine, a month of smiles, and best of all: a month of Princess Aven And Prince Louis was, undeniably and irrevocably, in love.

He stood in front of the mirror, fixing his chocolate brown hair. He was- for the first time in a long while- excited to address his citizens.

A few minutes later, Demiars familiar face peeked through the door to his dressing room, before he leaned against one of the many carved grain wardrobes. He asked questions, and Louis answered in a way he was certain would appear interested- but in reality, Louis's mind was elsewhere.

"Everyone's excited to see you, Your Highness." Demiar told him, pleased to see that Louis was smiling again. It had been many dark years for the kingdom, yes. But those months had been dark for Louis too, and not just in regards to the weather. Demiar missed seeing his best friend's smile, and was fully prepared to relish in it every opportunity he got.

"Tell 'everyone' I'm excited to see them too. I'll just be a moment." Louis said, straightening his blue tie. Aven liked blue. "Is she ready yet?"

Louis didn't even need to utter her name anymore- Aven was the only person on his mind, so everyone else came to expect that she was who he was referring to.

"She's been ready for hours, it's just nerves stopping her from coming out."

Not too long after, he half walked- half skipped to the bottom of the grand staircase. Hours passed, or so it felt to him. In reality no more than 3 minutes ticked away, but reality always seemed to stretch for him when she was involved. As Aven finally emerged, he wished he'd had longer to prepare himself. Longer to breathe before she stole all his remaining breath away.

Aven's dress for the occasion was light blue, with slightly darker flowers embroidered on to the flowing skirt, which graced the floor with the lightness of the air itself. The diamond necklace- shaped like a heart- hung round her neck, shining in he beams on sunlight like no less than stars in the stained glass window's tint. Whilst the matching ring did the same- for him it meant more.

It meant love.

It wasn't the attire that stopped his heart,

though. It was her. She stopped, and started it over and over. It was hers, if she wanted it.

She reached up to tuck her snow-kissed hair behind her ears, and he admired her earrings- on theme, in the shape of sunshine. It made sense. After all- she was the one to restore sunshine to the kingdoms. She started to walk gracefully- fists balled and clutching the hem of her dress in bunches- but promptly gave way to a jog. As she met him at the bottom, she held his chin up with her hands, as though inspecting him.

"You sure do clean up good." She said teasingly, childish grin that she saw many years ago, plastered on her face and her nose scrunched up.

"You're not so bad yourself, Princess."

She raised a playful eyebrow.

"Not so bad? Is that supposed to be a compliment?"

"I would get down and ask you to marry me again, were you not already my wife."

"Nothing's stopping you."

Rolling his eyes, but playing along anyways-he dropped to a knee and reached into his pocket. He had a flower. It was not a ring- far from it- but it would do.

"Aven Laila von Lothbrok. Would you do me the upmost honour of becoming my wife¿'

"Hmm, I suppose you are rather handsome. And sweet. And you have good teeth. That's very important."

"Is that a yes?" He was as eager to get the answer -even if he did know wha it would be, both were clearly enjoying the futile game.

"It's a yes!" She beamed at him.

"We're newlyweds! Rejoice!"

"Does that mean we get a honeymoon?" She held in her giggle bursting to come out.

Rather than answering- he stood from his previous kneel, and held his hands to the sides of her face.

"Anything for you, my Aven." Hushed, barely even a whisper. "Anything at all."

He pressed a light kiss to her lips, butterfly-like.

"But right now, we have a party to attend to!" He pulled away, spinning her round to stand by his side as they began to walk- his hand resting around her shoulders and hers around his waist. Aven groaned at him, and he chuckled to himself- amused.

She tried to keep up the annoyed facade, but simply couldn't. She ended up grinning up at him as they made their way to the ball room, radiant as ever.

"Ready, Your Highness?" She said, smile still bright as ever. All suggestion of anxiousness had dissipated at the mere sight of him. She smiled down at her, practically melting into her steel grey eyes. Ironic, that the brightest person in his life could have such colourless eyes. Colourless- but not lifeless. They had more fire than perhaps any others he'd every seen.

"Of course I'm ready. I have you."

"You always will."

"Always?"

"Always."

Outside, the sun shone upon the rows of crops. It was a sight that they should've grown accostomed too, and yet they wouldn't for a long while. It was all so utterly dreamy. So perfect. The crops weren't just gouper berries anymore, hundreds of different fruits and vegetables scattered the place. Even flowers! Louis made certain to pick a bunch of jasmine everyday, and hand them to Aven without fail. An array of pinks, blues, reds and yellows swarmed the area, as though a rainbow had eaten away the snow. The only white left in sight was that which of Aven's hair- curled in graceful waves down her back. Louis had never loved the colour of snow more.

Just beyond the castle wall, group of children lay, crafting daisy chains besides a fruit stall.

The stalls twisted into a circle formation, with an opening for the castle at one end and an elevated platform at the other. Catherine and Silas stood, situated behind the platform. Both were preparing to head onto the stage, and both were acting far more poised than they felt.

In amongst the centre of the celebration were the villagers dancing the national dance, singing (or screaming, depending on how hard one listened) the songs of their people.

The doors to the castle opened and the kingdom silenced itself, not requiring a word from anyone to know what to do. Heads turned and gasps followed, filling the warm summers air with surprise.

Light footsteps padded alongside Louis' as he and Aven made their way down the stone staircase. As they walked- their eyes met with those of the villagers. Smiles all around. It was freeing. They felt free! There was such a difference, Aven thought, from the beginning of the marriage to now. From mere months earlier to then. Her world was no longer her own, she shared it with Louis happily. She had fallen in love, and he had a second shot at it.

"6 year old me would be so proud." Louis muttered under his breath, so only she could hear. She giggled in response.

"Oh yeah?"

"I liked you back then too." A blush coloured her cheeks, as she grinned to herself.

The couple walked past the kids crafting bracelets of daises, and one of them reached up to hand Aven a flimsy daisy chain, Aven thanked the child, whilst Louis took her wrist gently, and tied it on. They all watched as the overjoyed child skip away- to ramble to his mum about the couple.

They walked-with purpose- hand in hand towards the stage. As they reached the wooden platform, both clearing their throat as they do so- Louis took the piece of paper they had written earlier that day and placed it on a stand on stage. Though the crowd was packed, all eager to hear what ever they have to say, they buzzed with the thrill of the noise- Louis was heard loud and clear as he started to speak.

"We're dreadfully sorry to interrupt your festival today, but if it's okay with you all, we'd like to make a speech."

Cheers and claps broke out from the crowd

before Aven smiled, and hushed them.

"Louis and I did not marry for love."

Some people nodded, some looked ove at loved ones puzzled. Some had speculated since the start, and now wore similarly smug expressions.

"AT FIRST¡' Aven continued, "We truly are in love now. Head over heels, ankles over chest- whatever. He is my husband, and will remain that way for as long as he can put up with me."

Louis took over. "We had been struggling with the snow for years, and it seemed never to end. However, this marriage brought us all the hope that summer may return. The marridge brought everything it needed too in the end, and as in added bonus- Aven and I fell in love while we were at it."

They both looked at each other, squinting their eyes from the sunshine that rain apon them . There was no denying that they were in love. All could see it, every citizen, guard, and troll. The cheer- ing continued, before breaking into a round of the natonal anthem yet again. The two royals walked from the platform and made their way onto a guarded bench-still grasping each others hand tightly- just as Queen Catherine and King Silas walked onto the platform. Though they were sure that speeches followed- neither heard,

Both were too preoccupied with each other, too preoccupied with love.

"Princess, " Louis whispered, "My Aven. My princess."

"What's wrong?"

"Nothing. Nothing's wrong at all."

He was wondering how on earth he got so lucky

A wedding; a joyous occasion for all, maybe not at first, but they had never been happier.

A joyous occasion for all indeed.

Printed in Great Britain
by Amazon

22747586R00136